MW01698096

A Hidden Danger

by Nicole Marie Woodcock

Background of the cover is by Joshua James Imagines work title: The Horizon

The details on the front and back cover are designed by Laura Luikhart.

Book Layout © 2016 BookDesignTemplates.com

A Hidden Danger by Nicole Marie Woodcock – 3rd.

Third printing edition 2021.

ISBN: 978-1-7369853-0-4

This book is dedicated to Mr. Mark Williams.

He believed that if you set your mind to do something, then you can do or be anything you wanted to be. Thank you, Mark, for believing in me and teaching me to reach for the stars. You will be missed by all who you have touched in this life.

To my dear readers,

Trigger Warning: There will be mentions of emotional and verbal abuse, physical harm to people, kidnapping, and sexual abuse. If you have ever been affected by any of these, please proceed with caution if you are sensitive to these situations, know you are not alone, and you are a survivor—even when others don't believe you. A Hidden Danger isn't intended for anyone that is underage due to the graphic nature and details within this book.

Sincerely,

Nicole Marie Woodcock

PRELUDE

Legends have always been a part of our world. Part of the stories that we've heard told through the ages of every culture and in many native tongues. Does it make you wonder if these legends held a spark of truth to them? It should. For if parts of the stories are real, could new legends and myths be born in every generation? If so, one such story has already begun.

Across the many lands and seas, there is a place called Emerald Green. This beautiful land held a rich history, and many legends run deep within its foundation. One such story will continue to grow with the ripples felt for generations to come. The part of the story that we are interested in starts in the year 1834, and not at its beginning entirely, as you will later discover, dear reader.

CHAPTER ONE

Just outside Emerald Green, known as Ireland, at twilight, in the remote countryside, there was a manor. The manor's lower floors were well lit, while the upper floors were dark; the sounds of music and a party drifted through the air. A beautiful, curved wooden staircase captured everyone's attention as the centerpiece of the entryway.

Halfway up the stairs sat a girl who had tripped and fallen, her body still, arms crossed on a stair. Her right cheek rested on her arms as tears trailed down her face. The girl in question just turned sixteen years old. Her eyes were a beautiful dark brown with green and gold accents. Her face was round with high cheekbones, a broad forehead, and a button-shaped nose. Her long, dark brown hair mixed with strands of light red trailed halfway down her petite frame. She was small and thin, weighing about seven stone, or ninety-nine pounds.

The upper part of her hair was styled into a beautiful bun, and the rest hung down loosely. The dress she wore was beautiful and unusual; she made it herself for her sixteenth birthday. The color of the dress was a pearl pink with a shallow, round neckline, short puffed sleeves, an empire-style waistline, and a floor-length skirt. Sown into the silk of the dress was a beautiful pattern, and on her feet were a soft pair of white slippers.

Down below the stairwell, a door opened, and several figures, speaking in hushed tones, moved to the entrance hall. The only man in the group went out the front door and closed it behind him. The two females were parting ways as well. The younger woman hurried down a side hall, opened the entrance to the servant's staircase, and disappeared. The older woman turned to the girl on the stairs. Her eyes glistened with concern as she cursed the girl's family under her breath.

She knew Ailene, the girl's grandmother would be rolling in her grave to see how much worse things had become for the child since coming back here. In many ways, she felt she failed the young lady in question.

Matthew and Martha had gone way too far this time, and it made her blood boil. With a steady pace, she knelt beside the girl on the stairs and rubbed a soothing hand across her back. The child's tears slowed to a sniffle as she looked up. She helped the young girl up and wrapped her in a tight embrace, whispering comforting words to her.

Ten minutes later, a voice was heard. "Aine?"

The older woman looked up. "Yes, Quinn?"

"David is back with a couple of others and is in the kitchen."

Aine nodded. "We will be down. Go to my room and grab the items off my bed."

"Yes, ma'am." The girl scuttled away.

"It's time," Aine murmured to herself as she pulled the crying teen up and carefully steered her down the stairs and into the kitchen. David and a few men turned and looked at them as they entered the kitchen.

They stood in silence for what seemed like a lifetime. Quinn came back with the items, handing an envelope to Aine first.

Aine, in return, gave it to the child. She then took the dark green velvet cloak from Quinn and settled it around the girl's shoulders and pulled the hood up.

Aine smiled gently at her to ease her fears, for this was the start of the last plan that should have happened a few years back. "I have been selfish, me girl, for I should have followed yer grandmother's wishes well before this. I have grown to love ye like ye are me own daughter. It is for this reason, and others I have not done me legal duties towards ye."

“What? That isn’t true, Aine.” While the girl’s voice was soft and child-like, it held an expression of confusion and bewilderment, much like her face.

Aine ignored the girl and continued. "Ye are leaving tonight for a safer place, away from our homeland what ye need inside this envelope. Ye are special and worth more than ye realize me, dear. Ye are loved, never forget that."

The young girl raised an eyebrow, her lips twitching as she fumbled for the words. "But I'm not. If I was then things would be different from what they are!” She stomped her foot and crossed her arms.

Aine raised her eyebrows at the young girl. She had been raised better than that and placed her hands on her hips. "Do ye remember what yer grandmother told ye, Jessica, on yer eighth birthday?" Aine asked.

"She said she favored me."

Aine nodded. "That ye are, ye are loved and cherished. It might not seem like ye are. Ye are truly loved."

Jessica touched the small necklace around her neck. The pendant was a golden cross with vines etched around the edges to form a border with runes engraved on it. The center held a sparkling rose. She glanced down at the necklace for a time then looked up, her gaze moving around the room and noting David's absence before settling back onto Aine.

CHAPTER TWO

David left the kitchen, letting the two women talk uninterrupted. He had more important things on his mind. He passed through the main entrance and headed toward the ballroom. The strains of muffled music seemed too cheerful for the plan taking place in the kitchen. With a shake of his head, he turned to the door a few feet away from the ballroom and stepped inside. The strains of music muffled as he entered the room and closed the door behind him.

The moon cast its light across the darkened area, but David hurried across the room with ease, stopping once he reached the safe. He crouched down and inhaled a few shaky breathes, flexing his fingers as he studied the lock. David closed his eyes and tried to remember the combination he'd seen his employer do while he'd watched from his vantage point by the bookcase as he'd fixed a broken shelf six months ago.

David reached out and placed his hands on the lock and closed his eyes, trying to bring that day to clarity and started to turn the lock. Time seemed to slip, and he became nervous. Sweat glistened from his brow and he prayed for a miracle. He had been gone too long already.

The lock clicked open on the fifth try. David released the breath he didn't realize he'd been holding and grabbed the money inside. He took out the cash and closed the safe. David folded up the money and placed it inside his pants pocket. He walked out, freezing in the doorway as his eyes landed on Matthew, his boss, standing outside of the door.

"What are you doing?" His tone was cold as steel.

Before David could come up with his answer, a female voice shouted down to them. "Quinn found our young mistress outside sitting on a bench!"

The two men turned and looked down the hall at the sound. Relief flooded David's face as he called back. "Thank you, Susan!"

David put on a concerned expression to mask the fortune of his narrowed escape.

“Some of us were looking for our young mistress since she left the party early, sir."

David watched Matthew nod his head with narrow eyes. When Matthew didn't say anything, David flashed a faint, apologetic smile and walked away. David paused as he heard another approach from behind, and then the voice of his employer's wife filled the air.

"Don't worry, dear, soon we will not have to worry about our youngest or that foolish woman. Come back to the party. We are just starting the toasts."

David kept walking, sneaking a glance over his shoulder to see Matthew put a hand on his wife's lower back and guide her to the party.

Perhaps Aine was right. It was time to get Jessica out of here so he and Aine could quit their services here too. They were only here for the girl and nothing more.

As David rounded the hall corner, he paused by Susan’s side. “Thank you again,” he whispered.

The older woman smiled sadly. "As long as you get the girl away from here successfully, I can retire in peace.” She turned and walked away.

David made his way back to the kitchen. As he stepped through the doorway, he noticed Jessica fiddling with her pendant. "Everything set? he asked.

"For the most part, yes," responded Aine.

Turning to the group of men who stood silently waiting, Aine smiled. "Thank you, Alroy, for doing this for us, and thank you all for helping her."

"No, thank you is needed. The girl's grandmother and grandfather were my parents' dearest friends, and I will see the girl to safety. Make no mistake about it."

"We know," said David, stepping over to Jessica. He took the envelope from her and placed the stolen money inside before giving it back to her.

"Please don't make me go," Jessica pleaded.

"You have to," David said.

Everyone proceeded through the back door that led into the garden from the kitchen, down the path towards the gates. They moved quietly, so they didn't alert the dogs. The group split off into two upon reaching the gate. Aine and David gave Jessica a hug and kiss before pushing her through with the men. Then they shut the gate and locked it.

Alroy pulled Jessica away gently. "They will miss you too, young lady. There isn't a choice; it isn't safe for you anymore."

Alroy helped Jessica climb into the front of the cart. He watched his companions load her luggage and climb into the back; weapons ready. Alroy jumped up into the seat beside the young lady, and with a slap of the reins, the cart jolted forward. The first part of their journey could be dangerous.

Alroy felt the girl was fearful, and she sat stiff as a board with her delicate hands, gripping her cloak. He offered no words of reassurance for there were none. His attention focused forward as they moved out onto the street. The only sounds heard along the gravel road were the horse's hooves, the wind, and Jessica's quiet sobs.

CHAPTER THREE

By the time they reached Port Lairge, it was midnight, and Alroy glanced at the sleeping girl who cried herself to sleep with a sad and heavy heart. Once they reached the stables, he climbed down slowly and stretched stiff muscles before finding a blanket for the girl.

They unhitched the horses and handed them over to a stable hand. A few minutes later, the stable boy came back with some fresh horses. Alroy watched the few men he had a stand at the ready with guns raised and prepared for any trouble.

"Sir, you are taken care of."

Alroy turned and looked at the young hand and gave him a few coins. "We were never here."

The boy nodded his head gravely. Alroy turned his attention to his men and gave a sharp whistle. They moved back to the cart and boarded quickly. It was around the twenty- a five-mile mark that they stopped and got off the wagon and moved into the nearby field.

Under a grove of trees, they made a small campfire, cooked up some food, and offer it to the girl. Jessica refused the meal and pulled her knees up to her chest and rested her chin on them. She was so overwhelmed; she couldn't even acknowledge her companions.

Jessica was angry and afraid. *Angry because the two that she loved most sent her away with little explanation as to why. Jessica wondered if they ever truly loved her at all. Or was she so much a burden that they were better off without her? She was afraid and uncertain about what was in store for her now. She didn't know how to live on her own or what to do.*

By sunset, they had moved on, destroying any evidence they'd been there. The group reached Wicklow in the morning hours and checked into a hotel for the rest of the day.

Once Jessica was safely settled in her room, she got the water running in the tub for a bath. She froze when she heard a knocking on the door. She moved slowly over to it. "Who is it?"

"It's Alroy, milady." She opened the door a crack to check and then pulled it open more. "Yes?"

"One of the maids will bring you up some fresh clothes shortly."

Jessica frowned. "You didn't need to do that. I would have been fine..." Her voice trailed off into an unsure whisper.

"I wanted you to be comfortable for the last part of the journey, and a beautiful party dress wouldn't be it. Your grandmother would have killed me if you weren't taken care of."

Jessica swallowed. "I am sure she wouldn't have, but thank you."

He nodded and walked away.

She closed and locked the door. Jessica made her way back to the tub and shut off the water. She took off her shoes and stockings, and as she started to remove her dress, a knock sounded at the door. She froze in mid-movement before bringing the straps back up and moved back to the door.

"Who is it?"

"I have some clothes for you, ma'am."

Jessica unlocked the door and opened it. The girl was a few years older than her. Jessica reached out for them and took them from her. "Thank you."

"Is there anything else I can do for ye?"

"No." Jessica paused for a second as the maid started to turn. "Wait, do you have anything I can pull my hair back with?"

The maid thought for a second. "I have some ribbon ties."

Jessica watched as the maid rushed off. She left the door open, turning back to the bed, and laid out the clothes. The chemise was cream-colored with long sleeves that flowed openly at the end like a trumpet shape while the overdress was a deep red with lovely trim lacing up the front of the chest.

"Ma'am?"

"You may come," Jessica responded as she turned to meet the girl.

The maid handed her the ribbons.

"Thank you."

"You're welcome." The maid left the room closing the door behind her.

Jessica locked the door and spun around. Removing her clothes, she slid down into the warmth of the water and let out a sigh as tears and anger flooded her again. *The man had been thoughtful for taking care of her comfort. She knew it would be short and was filled with uncertainty about what will become of her after Alroy and his friends left her.*

After a time, she got out and pulled a bath sheet around herself, moved to the bed, and fell asleep.

Jessica jolted awake as a loud, pounding noise filled the room.

"Are you alright, milady?" Alroy asked through the door.

"I am," she called out, her words strained with weariness.

"It's time to go."

"Give me a minute." She rapidly pulled on her undergarments and the overdress. After slipping on her shoes, pulling her tangled hair back, and throwing on the cloak, Jessica grabbed her old dress and followed Alroy outside to the cart.

By the next afternoon, Jessica found herself at Dublin's port. Upon reaching the docks, Alroy pulled the horses to a stop and got off the cart. "Stay here. I will be back soon."

Jessica waited nervously for Alroy to come back. She heard the sound of clicking guns and prayed feverishly. Jessica let out a relieved sigh when she spotted Alroy coming back towards her. He climbed up beside her and with a slap of the reins, had them moving again. Jessica noticed Alroy pulled the horses to a stop halfway down the docks.

He jumped out and helped her down before shouting up to the ship, asking to speak with the captain.

The sound of running feet became louder. She felt Alroy's fingers on her hands; they were rough but warm like David's, and her heart ached for him and Aine. She pushed her thoughts away and composed herself as she watched him pull out a ticket and paper that were clipped together from the folder given to her by Aine. Two men came into view.

The taller of the two men spoke. "I am the captain of this ship. What is it you need?"

When Alroy didn't respond, she glanced nervously at him as he silently handed over the papers to the captain. The captain took them, and by the light of the lantern, read them carefully.

He looked up. "So, my secret stowaway?"

Alroy nodded. "She will be kept safe?"

It was both a statement and a question. The captain nodded. "Yes. She will be safe aboard my ship; make no mistake."

"What of the rest of the trip?"

"Others will be waiting and seeing her to the destination."

Alroy seemed satisfied as he turned and gave the girl a small comfort squeeze to the shoulder.

The captain issued an order for his man to get the bags. He motioned for the girl to follow him. He turned to her. "My name is Captain Dylan. My cabin is just down the first hall." He offered her his arm. "If you need anything, let me know. You are safe here, and no harm will come to you."

CHAPTER FOUR

Jessica and the captain reached her door and waited. In the dim light of the hall, she made out two shipmates approaching with her bags. They placed them into the room and moved back up the passageway. Jessica stepped inside, looking around at the simple cabin.

The door shut behind her as the captain left. She pushed the hood of her cloak back and turned around in a slow circle, taking in the room. A single narrow bed was placed along the far wall while a small desk with a lamp and a chair sat a few feet away. There was a small sink and pot beside it.

Moving toward the table, she lit the lantern, watching the light chase away the shadows. She walked toward the bed and sat down. Unsure of the contents, the envelope felt heavy to her. With awkward, trembling fingers, she opened it and emptied the contents onto the bed. She noted different size papers and money. She hesitantly began to count the money and realized there was £200 total.

She blinked in surprise and recounted it a couple more times to make sure she was not making a mistake. She clenched the money tightly until her knuckles were white. *How did David come by this large a sum? Did it even matter? Did she want to know? It wasn't like she could do anything about it now, could she?*

She placed the money back into the envelope, picking up the folded paper and the one that was sealed. Taking the folded paper first and opening it, she recognized Aine's handwriting as she began to read it.

Me girl,

I have pondered over so many things in the last few months to say to ye, but I never could find the words to express my thoughts. I fear now I have run out of time. Ye are growing up so beautifully. I know ye don't see it, but ye are, and when the time comes, ye will open up into the most beautiful flower of them all.

I suffered in shame, for I feel that I failed yer grandmother, and now I genuinely believe I failed ye too. I am deeply sorry. I have been selfish, and I did ye wrong by keeping ye close. I should have sent ye away as instructed by yer grandmother sooner than what I am doing now.

Yer grandmother was a good and kind woman. I feel that you will be even higher than her. This journey will be a new start for ye, take it, embrace it, and live it to the fullest that ye can.

My blessing for ye is this: May the protection of the Lord keep ye safe and His light to guide ye. May a new sunrise bring ye a renewal of hope and joy and love to fall upon ye. Until our next meeting.

Always in my heart and prayers,

Aine

p.s. David gives his love.

Jessica blinked back tears as she kissed the paper and put it back into the envelope. Picking up the last one, she noticed the parchment seemed old, and she broke the seal on it. She opened and stared in astonishment at the old handwriting and began to read it.

22 July 1826

Dear Wildflower,

I hope you never have to read this, but if you are, then I am not in your life anymore, child. And I never did finish your training or see you grow into a young lady. A grandmother should never have favorites, but you were mine, sweet child. There's so much I want to tell you, but the timing isn't right. However, the answers will come in time.

I have taken you from my son and his wife, for the pure loathing and hatred I saw directed at you. Had made me fear for your safety my Wildflower.

The only clue I had that you were different as I watched you grow in the first couple of years, was your face and eyes. Your hair color was the darkest I have ever seen or even remember running in our family. It seemed to me that you belong to another race. That within it started my questioning and concerns in regards to your mother and her past.

My son refused to speak about it, and when he came back with her as his wife from America, I made a trip to the Americas myself to see what I could uncover about your mother. My efforts were unsuccessful.

I could find nothing on your mother within those years, and my suspicions were growing. I began to wonder if your mother truly was who she claimed to be. I did not have proof nor evidence that supported my theory. Nonetheless, I did not leave empty-handed. I did discover a clue, and you, my dearest, were the reason I walked away with a small truth.

A gentleman, if he could be called one, had seen my picture of you as I studied it and rudely asked who you were, and I told him you were my granddaughter. A guarded look came across his face, and his voice held an edge to it. "Looks to me like a savage Indian," he said to me. I bristled at his words and told him to leave my presence, and he did.

With that small bread crumb of an answer, I had come home and pulled you away from your parents. By this point, I would have chosen you already for being the favored one, child. I will not state more, for it isn't safe. My dear granddaughter, you are a beautiful princess, and you are our hope and future.

Never lose your faith in the Lord, child, be brave, and in time, the right people will be brought into your life to help and protect you. When that time comes, know that I love you more than anything in this world besides our Lord. You are and will always be the greatest gift that He has given me, and I am genuinely thankful for each passing day.

Be kind, have courage, and love always.

With much love, your grandmother,
Ailene

Jessica dropped the paper. It fluttered to the floor and landed at her feet. She looked up and stared straight ahead, not daring to believe what she had read. Thoughts drifted in and out of her mind. *How could it be? Was it even possible? What did it mean? Why would her mother be ashamed of her family? Or was Martha her mother after all or what of her father? Was he not her father?*

They ran in a circle around her mind, and she picked up the letter and put it back into the envelope with the rest of the items. She noted there were passports and visas to different places that she assumed would be needed.

Jessica stood and placed the envelope on the table. She kicked off her shoes and walked back over to the bed, collapsing into the mattress from exhaustion. As soon as her head touched the pillow, sleep overtook her senses and mind. The ship left the dock and started Jessica on her journey away from the home she ever knew.

CHAPTER FIVE

Within a couple of hours, the ship reached its stop in Holyhead, in Aglesey, Wales. Jessica had awakened to some harsh and worried tones outside her door before a rapid knock sounded. By the time Jessica had pushed herself up into a sitting position, the captain had come in and motioned to a couple of men to grab her things. He pulled Jessica up to her feet, grabbing her cloak and putting it around her.

"I will be sending you across the land to our next stop."

"Wait, why?"

The captain and his first mate glanced at each other before looking at the girl. He took a deep breath and let it out slowly.

"Something has come up, and I've promised to keep you safe. I wasn't expecting to be boarded and searched, and since I normally don't take passengers, it might raise questions."

She nodded her head in understanding. She watched the captain's men take her belongings, and she followed them off the ship and onto the dock. They helped her onto a carriage heading to Amlwch, a twenty-one-mile journey. It proved uneventful, and they rented rooms at the nearest inn once they arrived. At sunrise, they traveled back to the ship, avoiding the dock inspection and setting sail once again.

After a few hours of resting, Jessica made her way up to the deck. She leaned against the railings and looked out over the water. Jessica stood motionless, trying not to think about the letter and the questions it raised. But she was already homesick, wishing she could run back to Aine and David.

How far will I have to travel? What's going to happen when I finally arrive? Jessica took a deep breath and tried to focus on the calming sound of the waves. *Why don't Aine and David love me anymore? Am I worthless? Oh, Lord, I can't do this. I don't want to do this. I'm so scared, please help me, Jesus.*

Her thoughts were interrupted by the sound of someone clearing their throat. Turning her head to the left, she saw one of the crew.

"The captain would like to see you, miss, when you have a moment."

Jessica nodded and turned to look out over the water again for a few minutes as his footsteps faded into the distance. Sighing softly, she turned and made her way across the deck. She stepped inside the door that led to the hall where the sleeping quarters were. She made her way down the hall, pausing outside the captain's door. Her hand froze before she could knock as Jessica heard him speaking to another voice that was soft and heavily accented.

"My brethren and I will make sure the woman will get to her destination safely."

"I will have my ship go at max speed that will put us at an early arrival time if the weather holds and buy you some time."

Feelings of concern and confusion flooded through her, and biting her lip, she knocked on the door. A moment of silence passed, followed by a scraping of a chair and footsteps. As the door opened, she spoke. "You wanted to see me, Captain Dylan."

"Yes, Miss McKinney. Akeem, that will be all."

"Aye, Sir." The six-foot man with a scar on the right cheek nodded as he left and shut the door behind him.

Dylan motioned for her to sit. She walked over to the chair, sweeping the skirt of her dress down behind her as she sat.

"There has been a slight change of plans."

"I am sorry, but I don't really understand what is going on."

Dylan raised an eyebrow. "They didn't tell you the route you would be taking?"

"They forgot that little detail."

"Originally, we would have taken you straight to Egypt mixed with our normal stops." Dylan shifted uncomfortably. "With the last inspection we had, I'd feel much better if we traveled a different route for you. The crew member who just left will be escorting you off the ship at our next stop. Akeem will contact some of his kin, and they will make sure that you will get to your final destination safely."

"I will trust you at your word. I never traveled so far from home before."

"It's settled then?"

"Yes." She stood, and he joined her, escorting her to the door.

"Good day, Miss McKinney."

"The same to you, Captain Dylan."

She left his quarters, and the door shut behind her. She walked down the hall to her room and went inside. She crossed the floor, kicking off her shoes and stretching out on the bed. Within minutes, the gentle sway of the ship put her to sleep.

The weather held good for six days, and they made much progress. But by the seventh day, the weather changed for the worse, and it slowed them down. They reached Liverpool after eleven days at sea. Once Jessica disembarked, she sat on a nearby bench.

With the sun mid-high in the sky, Akeem came with six men and motioned Jessica to follow him. They made their way into town, and upon reaching the hotel, they went inside.

Jessica didn't have time to take in her surroundings. She was quickly ushered up several flights of stairs and down a hallway to a suite of rooms.

She sat in an armchair near the window, dozing off in the warm sun. She blinked her eyes rapidly when she felt a rough shake. She glanced up at Akeem.

"We need to leave."

Upon reaching the streets, the roar of a massive fire greeted them. Jessica coughed as ash floated through the air. Several buildings were ablaze, and panicked shouts rang out with the sounds of gunshots. Bodies lay in the street, their terrified expressions frozen.

Jessica closed her eyes and tried to look away, but everywhere there were signs of killing and hysteria. The girl soon found herself in the center of a wall of men as they waited in the shadows.

Sounds of a cart and horses approached from behind them in the darkness. Jessica peered in between Akeem and another shorter man. She realized that one of Akeem's brethern, a stocky fellow, was driving the cart. They quickly loaded everything and helped her into the back, pushing her down and covering her with a blanket. The cart lurched forward as they departed.

CHAPTER SIX

Once they reached London, they found some lodging for the night and by the next morning, moved on to Southampton. They reached the city at nightfall and stayed in an inn. Sunrise of the next day, they headed for Gasport, and from there, their passageway was to Le Havre, France, by a ship that will sail on Wednesday.

The group found a hotel and stepped inside. A sense of home filled Jessica as a warm feeling surrounded her. The hotel was run-down, and a tired-looking man stood at the front counter. He perked up when he saw he had some guests. They booked a couple of rooms, and the man had a skip in his step as he showed them to their rooms.

Unlocking one door and stepping inside as he opened it, he showed Jessica her room first with a beautiful looking view of the waterfront with a small balcony. She turned to the man. "Thank you. It is beautiful."

A broad smile lit up his face, and the years seemed to drift off of him. "Thank you, lady."

He walked out of the room; two of her companions sat her luggage inside of her room.

Jessica turned and closed the door with a soft click. She slowly removed her cloak and let it fall behind her onto the floor. Jessica moved gracefully and looked out the balcony doors. Jessica leaned her forehead against the glass and stared out over the street. She lost all sense of time.

It wasn't until her legs felt numb from being in the same position, that she moved to the bed and laid down. She hugged one of the pillows to herself, curled into a ball, and fell asleep.

The next day seemed to drag by for Jessica, who just paced endlessly. She refused to eat or drink. She felt on-edge, and her heart was racing. By that evening, she left the room and went to the front desk, asking the man there where her companions' rooms were at.

"Four doors on the left-hand side."

"Thank you." She turned on her heel and quickly made her way back up the stairs to her floor. Going past her room, she counted the doors. She went to knock but heard harsh voices from inside. She couldn't make out the mumbled words, and she bit her lip unsure if she should disturb them or not. She lowered and raised her hand a few times against the worn wood of the door.

She inhaled deeply and exhaled harshly before shaking her head and moving away. She quickly walked back down the hall to her room locked herself inside again.

Jessica took only a few steps from the door when a knock sounded through the quiet room. It startled her and she jumped. "Who is it?"

"It's Akeem, miss."

Jessica took in a necessary breath of air she didn't realize she needed and moved back to the door and opened it.

"Did you need something? I saw you moving back down to your room."

She looked at Akeem and nodded her head slowly. "I wanted to know if it's possible to go see some shops tomorrow?"

He frowned for a moment as he thought. Jessica shifted slightly on her feet and held her breath.

"Only for a short time. One of the others will be escorting you, and you will do as your told."

"Of course," she reassured him, and he nodded his head and left.

The night seemed to drift quickly, and so did the morning of the second day. It was just after lunch that Jessica found herself in a shop browsing at their goods. But all too soon, the edgy feeling she had the other day was back and much stronger. She didn't like it. She took a step back and bumped into someone unexpectedly.

Jessica turned to face the person and started to apologize; the words died on her lips. Jessica realized the man was staring at her pendent intensely. She reached up and gripped the pendant in her hand tightly.

Her action broke the man's focus, and he moved his eyes up to hers, "Where did you get that beautiful pendant?"

Something inside her very being screamed at her not to answer and find her companion. She darted around the stranger and moved quickly down the aisle. Then the next. She made her away through groups of people when she spotted the escort with the stocky build and hurried over to him. Frantically, she told him what happened. He didn't respond but grabbed her arm firmly with narrowed eyes as he saw the fear in her state.

He moved quickly with her to the back of the store and out to the alley. They turned down so many streets that she didn't even bother trying to keep them straight in her head. The man's pace slowed down slightly as he entered a home.

Jessica looked around at the small but cozy kitchen, it was a simple one and nothing like the in her parent's home.

"Sit." Jessica looked toward the small kitchen table with a chair that was pulled out, and she moved the few steps to the chair and sat down.

He left the room. Some time had passed when a woman and six small children came into the kitchen without a word, followed by three boys her age. Not long after, the stocky man was back with a middle-age balding man, and they both looked grim.

They had conservation in their native language, and Jessica thought it sounded beautiful. Five minutes later, the stocky man turned to her grimly. "She will make sure that you will get back with the others and to deliver a message."

"Are you not coming?"

"No. We will not meet again."

She nodded her head and had a feeling that this was somehow her fault. She didn't notice the woman approaching her until she felt fabric being draped around her shoulders.

She looked at the woman, who covered her head with the shawl and wrapped it under her chin. She tossed the ends over the opposite shoulders and tucked in any stray locks of hair. She fluffed the fabric slightly to hide Jessica's face. Soon after, Jessica was ushered out the door by the woman and her children.

After walking for some time, Jessica tried to take in the city since she had never been here before. The buildings varied in size, style, and function. The streets were wide or narrow depending where they went, and small trees dotted them in different places. She tried to take in much of her surroundings.

They reached the hotel, and the woman looked at Jessica. Jessica was puzzled as to why they had stopped, but the woman was making a shooing motion at her and saying a few words in her language. After a moment, Jessica realized that she was to lead the group now.

She turned and made her way inside and up the stairs to the next floor. Again, her steps led her to pass her door and down to her companions'. This time she raised her hand and knocked with determination. Sounds of footsteps were heard, and the door started to open, and she met the eyes with Akeem. She stepped aside and introduced him to the woman and her children.

They spoke for a moment in the same language Jessica heard earlier. Soon after, she bid farewell to Jessica and quickly departed with her children.

"Don't leave your room or turn on the lights," Akeem ordered.

Before dawn on the nineteenth of November, Jessica found herself being hustled through the streets to the docks and onto a ship that would carry them to Le Havre, France.

Once inside her room, Jessica started to look through her baggage. One bag had her favorite clothes inside; the second had some of her accessories and a couple pairs of shoes. The third had some of her books, and the smallest and last case held her teddy bear and the homemade blanket that her grandmother made her with a few knick-knacks. She removed the blanket and teddy and closed the case and set it down on the floor and crawled onto the bed and fell asleep.

The days went by without incident. Jessica took the time to read or wrote in her diary. *I sit here in my room on another ship. I went from being a stowaway to a passenger. My whole being is filled with uncertainty still. The anger I felt has ebbed away into sadness and heartbreak. I feel like something is not right with any of this, dearest diary. And yet I feel like I can sleep for a thousand years and still feel like I am weighed and pressed down by a stone. I have taken to crying when I am awake. My emotions are too much, and all I want to do is scream and never stop. I have traveled over thousands of miles, and the end is not yet in sight.*

Always, Jessica

The days drifted by slowly. It wasn't until the eleventh day that the sky started to darken, the wind seemed to pick up sharply, and the men on the ship became jittery and uneasy. Jessica couldn't understand why until she heard a loud rumble in the sky. It seemed like the sun was closing in on itself, and the air grew chilly. Akeem moved her back into the room and closed the door. Soon the ship was tossed to and fro, fighting against the wind and waves.

It wasn't until three days later, that everything grew calm again. Jessica and Akeem ventured out and up onto the decks with a few others. Some of the crew were lost, and a couple of them hurt. The ship took on some minor damage. The crew of the ship nursed the ship for two days before arriving at the port of Leharve.

Soon after this, Jessica found herself inside a carriage heading to Paris. Within fifteen hours, they arrived, passing through the city quickly. Jessica hoped one day she could return. They reached the train station, and Jessica, after a few minutes, felt like she was being watched. She slowly looked around but couldn't find anyone looking at them. She fidgeted nervously, for the awareness was prickling at the back of her neck. Soon enough, Jessica found herself on the train, and a little under six hours, they came to Lyon for a brief stop and moved on. Jessica kept staring outside the window, watching the scenery going by and writing randomly in her diary as the words came to her.

Tears are running down her face, rushing like a river of heartbreak and despair. The lonely one cries out for the relief of the torments of her past. The sadness and anger she feels now.

These tears keep coming down her face rushing like a river of heartbreak and worthlessness. She cries out to God for help; to release the despair of mixed emotions she has. The tears are coming down her face like a flood, and towards the heavens.

Then and there, the young lady decides to start over, but she is still unsure about everything. She asks, 'Oh, God, why me?' Her soul, heart, and body scream out for the comfort and safety she needs.

The friendless one who no one notices. In the girl's world of solitude, the pain and all the hurtful words and deeds done shout endlessly at her.

The only comfort she has is knowing that the Lord always knows and understands fully what she needs. Her Lord's caring is more profound than any part of the heavens and more significant than the earth. His comfort is what she needs, and He gives it freely.

The tears of heartbreak and loneliness she will bury until the next outpouring. No one will see, besides God, His angels, and the saints.

Seven hours later, Jessica finally closed her diary and found herself, disembarking in Monaco, Switzerland. There they took to another ship to Cecino, Italy, in twenty-seven days.

From there, she found herself on another train and traveled roughly four hours to Rome. They stayed three days to rest and for the men to figure out their next move.

Jessica couldn't understand what was going on, nor could she realize why they were so afraid. She noticed the weapons for the first time although they'd been in plain sight, and that had her worried. It was an edgy feeling that had Jessica nervous and anxious. In the middle of the night, they left Rome and took the 142-mile journey to Napoli, from there to Bari, Italy, and catching a ferry to Durres, Alania.

It was during those nine hours that Jessica started to feel as though she was being watched again. She furrowed her eyebrows and looked around, trying to find the source. She noticed a handsome man across the ferry staring at her. She noticed, his dark hair blowing from the wind. His body was fit, and he seemed relaxed enough, talking to the person beside him who was facing the sea. Even so, Jessica couldn't help but feel frightened.

She made her way back to her companions, touching the arm of a man with a limp and greying hair. He turned to her and she said, "I think...," She shook her head. "No, I *feel* like someone is watching me."

The man stiffened at her words. He murmured something fiercely in another language before addressing Jessica's concerns. "Where?"

She pointed in the direction, and he nodded and moved away. It wasn't too long after that, the man returned and they moved to the rest of the group. He whispered a conversation between him and Akeem. The man stepped away and pulled a flintlock pistol from his person and moved away. No sooner than he left their view. The group quickly disembarked.

From Jorgucat, they caught a train to Athens. She managed to see some of the area before being ushered into a small house. She was pushed into a small room with no window or light, and she sat huddled as she heard the men's voices speaking low. They were loading guns, the clicking sounds rattled her.

She squeezed her eyes shut and started to pray that nothing abysmal will happen to them all. It was an intense feeling she didn't know how long she stayed in the room. She managed to find a chamber pot and emptied her bladder a couple of times.

It felt like ages to Jessica, but the door opened up and Akeem entered the room. She leaped off the bed and took her by her arm and out the door. The two hurried through the streets to the train station. Once there, they snuck onto the cargo car, just in time for the train to depart with a loud whistle. She turned and looked at him. "Where are the others?"

He frowned at the girl; his tone serious. "They are passengers on the train."

She bit her lip. "Where are we heading?"

"Peraias."

Satisfied with that answer, she chose not to ask anything more. She sat quietly and arranged herself on a well-worn steamer trunk. Akeem's eyes closed and she couldn't tell if he had fallen asleep or not. Either way, she didn't want to bother him, so she played with the fringe on her shawl, lost in thought. Eventually, the train slowed into the station; they jumped off and quickly moved into town.

They met up with the others, and she realized their group seemed to be getting smaller, but she didn't ask. They hurried through the many streets of Peraias, carrying the girl's luggage, never once stopping until they reached the seaport. They booked passage for the next day to Chania, Crete, before renting a room for the night.

Jessica stayed awake huddled on the bed most of the night, sleeping only a few hours in the early morning. Sneaking around checkpoints on the way to get to the boat proved stressful, but by noon the ship left the port without incident. The fifty-one days of traveling was easy going for a change, and they disembarked after a few hours of reaching the port of Chania.

From there, it was an eight-day journey to Tympaki. Jessica found herself on the second day in the late watches of the night leaving town. Jessica and her group moved down the steep rocky sides of the bank to the ocean's edge. There they took a raft that was waiting and paddled into the water.

After a mile, Jessica started to see an outline of a ship, and once they reached it, she realized it was Captain Dylan's ship. A wooden ladder was tossed over the side, and they ushered her up the rope. Her bags were hauled up with the rest of her party.

From there, the rest of the journey passed peacefully, and within thirty-one days, they reached Alexandria, Egypt. Arrangements had to be made for the final part of her trip, so Jessica was able to rest and relax for three days before making the journey of a hundred miles to Cairo. As the sun rose the fourth day, Akeem informed her it was time to part ways. By sunset, a small group of men and a woman with red hair and green eyes would meet her, and she would be safe.

Jessica sat on a bench near the port beside her luggage all day in the shade, trying to read. An old woman from a shop saw her and walked over to her with a wrapped sandwich and drink before hurrying away. Sunset fell, but no one came to greet her.

She waited for another hour, then left to rent a room, hoping the money she had would last her until her final stop and she could find employment. Tears blurred her vision as she watched out the window, waiting, praying, nothing had gone wrong.

CHAPTER SEVEN

It had been five months and six days that Jessica traveled from her homeland to Cairo, Egypt, and six months of desperately living on her own. Jessica's eighteenth birthday was a week away, and she found herself sitting on a street corner with knees drawn up and crying during a rainstorm. Without being able to find work, her money was running out, and she was feeling desperate.

She heard a horse coming up the street. Jessica looked up as the animal came to a halt in front of her.

"Do you need assistance?" the hooded rider asked.

Jessica shrunk into herself more without responding, fear gripping her like a rope. He jumped down from his horse without a sound, rain pelting his black-clad body. His cloak hung heavily down his back and water dripped from his hood. His shadow cast over her, as he stepped forward and pulled Jessica to her feet with a commanding grip. Her right hand flew up and slapped the man as hard as she could.

"I will not go anywhere with you!"

"You will." His forceful tone left no room for discussion.

She continued to fight him. In a desperate attempt to free herself, she kneed him in the groin as hard as she could.

Jessica took a couple of steps back and turned to run. Before she could step away, he caught her again. Her back was against his chest, and he locked her into place against him, wrapping his arm around her waist. She started to scream, but he quickly covered her mouth.

Jessica tried to bite the palm of his hand and couldn't. She struggled despite the hopelessness of the position she was in.

Harsh, foreign words rasped warmly against her ear despite the rain. She froze as she watched another man drop from his horse and move out of sight. She didn't know how long they stood there.

After what felt like forever, the man came back into view. In one hand he held her small carry bag; in the other, her hotel key. The man holding her issued another order, and the man with the key moved back to his horse, swung up, and left with a few others.

Still holding her, the man spoke against her ear. "If I remove my hand, you will remain silent?"

Jessica nodded her head quickly; he removed his hand from her mouth. Jessica and the man stood there for a moment before he moved them to the horses. Jessica still dug her heels into the ground, resisting.

"Where are you taking me?"

"To Midbar Shemesh," was the gruff reply.

"What is it?"

The man spun around, picked her up, and set her on his horse.

“It’s a city."

"But why?" Jessica was hysterical, and it showed in her face and voice.

"It's no good for a woman to be on her own, and you need help."

Jessica bit down hard on her lip, causing it to bleed as she sniffled. *I am terrified and scared. I know he is right. Can I even trust him?*

What do I do now? Jessica snapped out of her thoughts as she felt the man mount up behind her. He brought his arms around her, took the reins with one hand, and raised the other to signal his men.

With that command, the group moved out of the city. They moved to the east for a few minutes and halted. There they sat in the pouring rain.

Jessica had become cold from the rain. Her teeth chattered as she shivered, and she turned herself into the man trying to keep warm. A low whistle sounded in the distance. The man answered with a whistle of his own and a small group of men reappeared in the rain. They had gone to retrieve the rest of Jessica's belongings.

They traveled south-east for about two hundred miles. It took them eight days to reach the gates of the Midbar Shemesh. The city was about 500 hundred square acres in size.

The streets inside the city were cobblestone and dotted with lamps. The alleys were too narrow for a cart to fit through. The buildings were brick.

Jessica could make out some trees or plants sprinkled here or there but nothing in detail in the dead of night. They made many different turns before finally reaching the center of the city, which was square with a shaded area and a well in the center of it.

They moved clockwise around the square until they turned onto another street. At the end of the street, there was a private lane leading to a building. The man dismounted and pulled Jessica from the horse. He gripped her upper arm and ushered her up the stairs and inside the building. He proceeded past the reception desk, and up the stairs to the second landing. From there, he moved her down the hall. They stopped in front of a glass display case, dripping water on the floor, where he gave three sharp knocks on the door to the right-hand side of it.

Not a second later, a deep but soft voice called out, "Enter."

In an instant, the man pushed the door open and dragged Jessica into the room behind him. Stopping in front of a mahogany desk, he shoved her in front of him before letting go of her arm. As the occupant looked up from the pile of papers on his desk, she defiantly made a show of her distaste for the soaked, black clad man standing behind her. She'd been right; he did have a powerful build to him. In the light, he was just as broad and muscular as she perceived him to be on the corner. He pushed his hood back, and Jessica could see that he was handsome in a rugged way, with smooth, sun tanned skin and high cheek bones. His black hair was shoulder length and looked to have some dark curl to it; or would if it were dry. His dark brown eyes were serious and brooding, his lashes thick and his arched brows knit in irritation. He had a short, trim circle beard, that added to his looks rather than take away, like so many others she'd seen. He was taller than her she knew from earlier, but he definitely towered over her. If he hadn't treated her so horribly, she might have fancied him.

A scrape of a chair brought her back, her head snapped back to the older man as he rose from his seat, puzzled.

"What is going on?"

"The girl was in trouble and needed help."

The older man nodded his head and motioned for Jessica to take a seat. She did so stiffly, not sure what was going on. She knew she had trouble money-wise, but how did the stranger know, and what was going to happen to her now?

"Can you tell me your name and how you came to be in these lands?"

She stared at the older man. The younger man made her uncomfortable, and she refused to say a word with him in the room. She shook her head to say "No." Clasping her hands in her lap tightly, she kept her eyes and head down.

A few tense moments passed by before the door shut. Jessica glanced up at the older man slowly as he asked, "Now, can you tell me so that I can better help you?"

Jessica let out a breath of rushed air harshly. She took another breath in and out just the same way before saying, "My guardians sent me away for some reason. I don't know why and I don't understand."

The man nodded his head thoughtfully. "They didn't provide you with means to live?"

"They did, but it is running out." The reply was almost too soft for him to hear.

He moved from around his desk to the front and leaned against it.

"What is your name?" Jessica's lips pressed into a thin line as fear shone in her eyes. Seeing this, the man spoke, "My name is Elchanan Stern."

"Jessica Piper McKinney." She noticed a gleam in his eye that she couldn't decipher. She quickly looked away and focused on the wall behind him and the desk. At the sound of his voice had her attention back on him, "I will give you a lodging."

She went to protest, but he raised his hand to silence her. "I have extra rooms that are open and not being used. In the meantime, I will try to find you a family that will be able to adopt you. I am surprised you lasted as long as you did on your own."

He motioned her to follow him out of the office, as they made their way through the building. "This building is called *Archives of The Moon.* It is a museum. However, unlike other museums. We deal mostly with priceless artifacts that display artistic, cultural, historical or other such things. We do offer some small exhibits like that, but we deal mainly with ancient texts that have been lost or found on digs. We try to restore and decipher them.

"As you can see, they are displayed with information about them. Some texts are not on display and are locked in a room for different reasons. We also house a library for the city."

"Why are you telling me this?"

He stopped, and she nearly stumbled into him as he turned around and stared at her.

"I am telling you this because I am offering you employment."

"But why?"

Elchanan stared at her. "It is the right thing to do."

She swallowed nervously as she licked her lips before responding. “I accept.”

"Come, we will get your papers filled out." She followed him back upstairs to his office."

"Who was the man that brought me?"

"That will be Boaz, my son.”

She remained silent as they reentered the room, and he pulled out the necessary papers. She quickly filled them out. Once they were finished, they left the museum. He took her to his home and let her pick out a room. He gave her some blankets and a pillow, and they retired for the night.

CHAPTER EIGHT

Eight months found Jessica living with Elchanan and him finding a family who took her in as an adoptive child. The family in question were patrons of the museum. Mr. and Mrs. Clayden had two older children in their early thirties and mid-twenties. A boy who was called Brent and a daughter whose name was Leslie, respectively.

Four months into the relationship, the Clayden's parents died in an accident that left her and her adoptive siblings alone. It was during this time that she had wondered about her grandmother's letter and wanted to ask them for help with finding the answers to her questions. She never addressed them, but it lingered in the back of her mind.

In her current situation, she found herself, along with her adoptive brother and sister, under the curator's care in many ways. He helped them with the selling of their parent's home, minus the family home outside of London, which transferred to Leslie. The money from the sale of their parent's house divided between the three of them, and soon after that, Brent left. The two sisters only heard from him on occasion, and when they saw him, they could tell he had started to drink and engage in risky behavior.

Jessica and Leslie managed to live in a hotel that offered apartments for housing. Leslie threw herself into her work almost nonstop, combating the grief in her work at the museum. Jessica also worked at the museum while privately keeping up with her studies.

Presently, Jessica moved down the hall from the receptionist's area, with return books in her arms from a patron who was running late. Stepping inside the library, she moved to the desk and set the books down.

Jessica left them there and headed off in search of her sister.

As she turned a corner around a shelf of books, she saw Leslie on a ladder trying to reach across the aisle to the other side. Jessica stared at her sister with a raised eyebrow. A frown pulled on Leslie's face as she persisted in reaching across the aisle to the other bookshelf.

Jessica moved closer. "Sister! What do you think you are doing?"

Leslie looked down and smiled. "Putting books away."

"I can see that. But you are not being bright about it, which I know you are, by the way. You could hurt yourself or worse, and I will be left alone again."

Climbing down, Leslie pulled her into a hug as Jessica started to cry.

"I'm sorry, Jessica. I promise. Now dry those tears." She brushed them off the girl's cheeks. "Now, what can I do for you?"

"I placed a stack of books on the desk which need to be returned by one of our regulars," Jessica said, waving her hands in the air as she spoke. "The one fellow who is jolly all the time with the long beard that is partly braided. You know who I am talking about."

"I do, and I will take care of them. Head back before Curator Stern finds out you left your area again."

Jessica nodded and walked away only to stop at the doorway. Taking a deep breath, she shouted down to her sister. "No more stupid stunts!"

Leslie crossed her fingers. "Promise."

Jessica smiled. "Good."

She hurried the rest of the way out of the library and down the hall. Once she reached the main doors with the staircase leading up, she moved across the entrance to another room where the sunlight streamed in through the windows. For a moment, she was transported back in time to the window room of her grandmother's house.

It had been a beautiful chilly afternoon on her eighth birthday. She'd worn a white dress which her grandmother had made for her—she still had the same dress tucked away in a box. She remembered she didn't want to wear it for it was white, but her grandmother had insisted upon it. She wore no shoes on that chilly day, just white tights.

Her grandmother had been smiling from the doorway, watching her have fun spinning in circles and enjoying the way the dress flowed out around her as she did.

Her grandmother studied her, she remembered the thoughtful expression and softly spoken words. "My dearest, Wildflower. We need to work on your posture some more, my sweet. It's imperative to how others see you." Her grandmother had been pulled away moments later to finish up the party preparations.

> Jessica was still spinning in the window room, having fun when the maid came in with a crash. Jessica blinked. She didn't remember the maid crashing into

the room. Jessica spun around and saw a man hurrying up the stairs. It took Jessica a moment to process what she had just seen before she sprinted out of the room and up the stairs after the man. Halfway up, she shouted.

"Excuse me! But you can't just go where you please!"

“Matters of men are not for little girls.” The British man turned as he reached the landing.

Jessica reached forward to tug on his arm. "I am telling you. You are not allowed to be up here." The man jerked his arm away, and she took a step back.

He pivoted around and kept walking. "I am going to see the curator."

Jessica scowled at the superiority in the man's tone. "My employer, who also happens to be the curator, gave me orders under no circumstances was he to be disturbed."

The man glanced behind him with a raised eyebrow and shrugged. Jessica felt her skin flush as she grew flustered. "Please leave and come back tomorrow. Or better yet, I'll take your name and address and have him contact you."

The man ignored her and kept going. Jessica hurried after him. She grabbed his arm, "Did you not hear me? I said no one could interrupt him when he's in a meeting."

The man jerked to a stop, twisting his arm out of her grasp. “Go bother someone else, little girl.” He pushed her away.

Jessica huffed at the unconcealed disdain and impatience on the man's face. She hurried around him and stood in front of the meeting room doorway; arms outstretched in an attempt to block him from opening the door. "I told you, ‘No!’”

Her cheek stung as he slapped her and pushed her to the side. She struggled to catch herself. Hot tears welled up in her eyes and blurred her vision, but she refused to let them fall. She heard the door squeak open behind her. She scrambled to her feet, but it was too late. Silence fell over the meeting as the attendees all turned to look. She cleared her throat and managed a shaky apology. "I'm sorry, sir, I tried to tell him that you were busy, but he wouldn't listen."

Elchanan Stern stood up from his seat at the head of the table. His face held a mixture of anger and annoyance at being interrupted.

Men sat around the table, casually dressed with black pants and various dark colors for the shirts. The ages of the men ranged from the late twenties and upwards. Some turned in their chairs to see what was going on. Jessica managed to step into the room and pushed the snobbish man out of the way. She folded her arms across her chest. Her heart pounded in her ears as she nervously stood there with her head bowed.

The snobbish man opened his mouth to speak, but the head of the museum beat him to it. "It is fine, girl, but since you are here, get more water for the tea."

Jessica nodded, left quickly, and turned down the hall. She stood there, taking in deep breaths with her eyes closed. Jessica started to move again after a couple of seconds, turning into the workers' lounge. The lounge held a small icebox, a stove, a table with chairs, and a sink area. Jessica started the preparations for the tea. Jessica stared off into space, absently rubbing her cheek where the slap landed, and tears fell from her eyes. Jessica wiped them as the whistling of the kettle sounded in her ears. She grabbed the potholders and tea kettle, and another stray tear fell and hurried down the hall toward the meeting.

Jessica noticed nobody had moved from their positions and hurried to the sideboard while avoiding eye contact. She removed the lid to the teapot and poured the water into it, setting the kettle down on the potholder next to it before putting the cover back on. Jessica turned, resisting the urge to curtsy, but before she could exit the room, and leave th etension behind.

Elchanan broke the silence. "Come here for a moment, Miss McKinney."

Elchanan stern tone frightened her. Jessica's green skirt swished around her ankles with each step towards him. She clenched fistfuls of the fabric, eyes down, as she stopped in front of him.

"Dear child, can you tell me what happened?" His tone softened.

Jessica didn't respond. Her supervisor reached out and placed his hand under her chin and lifted it so he could see her face. Jessica refused to look at him. She felt his fingertips brush her cheek, and winced, realizing that man's slap must have left a mark behind.

"I see. You're dismissed for the day." His tone held a threatening note to it.

"Thank you." Jessica's barely audible words seemed to echo as she hurried from the room. Her eyes met the man's eyes for a brief moment as she passed him and shivered as the door shut behind her. Then she heard her employer's voice from behind the door.

"You have some nerve hitting her!"

"She's just a woman!" the snobbish man replied.

"I am the guardian of that young lady!"

Jessica ran down the hallway and the stairs. She didn't want to hear the rest of the conversation. By the time Jessica reached the bottom, she was trembling with emotion and found herself needing a hug from her sister. Jessica headed left and down the hall back to the library to see Leslie.

She got to the doors of the library and paused. Her sister wasn't alone. Jessica held her breath as she listened, but she couldn't make out the identity of the new speakers.

There was something about them that was familiar to her. She couldn't pinpoint it, and that made her nervous and a little afraid. Standing still, Jessica tried to make out what was being said. The sound of their footsteps was coming closer.

Jessica ran to the other side of the hall and touched a secret panel in the wall. It opened up, and slipped inside, the door closing behind her. Curator Stern had shown it to her, just in case she ever needed it. Now more than ever, Jessica was thankful he did as she heard the group of people exiting the library at that precise moment.

Leaning against the coolness of the door, Jessica closed her eyes and wondered *if it was her estranged family and if so, were they on vacation? Or did they somehow find her? She prayed it was the former. She couldn't handle listening to another conversation of any kind about herself right now.*

Jessica moved to the other side of the passageway and up the stairs. She opened the door at the end and stepped inside the curator's office. Kicking off her shoes, she grabbed a random book from one of the shelves and sat down in front of the fireplace. Jessica seized a book about the finding of the Rosetta Stone and the meaning behind it. She opened it to the first page and began to read. Jessica slowly lost herself inside the pages to take her mind off the events that happened.

CHAPTER NINE

The afternoon sun drifted into the evening, and the stars danced and twinkled across the sky. Jessica had fallen asleep in front of the fireplace, and the book she had been reading laid beside her. The sound of approaching footsteps bolted Jessica from her sleep.

Her eyes darted about the room as she scrambled to her feet, fumbling for her book and shoes. She crawled under the desk, shoving the book and her flats to a corner, before reaching out and pulling in the desk chair. The door opened and shut. Jessica held her breath. The footsteps slowly circled the room and stopped behind the desk.

Jessica pressed herself further back into the corner. The chair was moved out of the way. As Jessica was yanked out from under the desk, she lashed out in hopes of striking her attacker.

The person caught her wrists and held them down. "That's the second time you have hit me without cause," the man said.

She ceased her struggles. "Let me go right this second, Boaz!" He released his hold on her, and she took a few steps away from him. "How in the world was I supposed to know it was you! For all, I knew you could have been a thief, a murderer, maybe both!"

They both stared at each other, neither backing down. A heavy silence descended across the room.

Boaz sighed. "I was sent to find you."

"And you just happened to be there with him!"

"Have you forgotten that he is my father, and I was also at that meeting and would have gone to his home?" he said.

"I wasn't paying attention to who was at the meeting and wasn't. Forgive me!"

Boaz's eyes narrowed. "You need to learn some respect."

"Show me a reason to respect you, and I will." Jessica huffed, folding her arms across her chest.

Boaz softened his expression. "The only reason I am here is that a distraught woman came to the house and claimed to be your sister and that you were missing."

"Leslie. My adoptive sister." The defensiveness went out of her as she bit her lower lip in concern for her sister's state of mind. Boaz motioned for her to follow him and moved around the desk and toward the door. Jessica grabbed her shoes and slipped them on before trailing behind the man.

They moved through the darkened hallways of the museum and out the back door, pausing just inside the doorway. Boaz stood still, his eyes narrowing as he searched the area. Jessica saw his face in the dim light and turned and tried to see what he saw or thought he saw, but all she saw was shadows of the night. While Jessica searched the darkness, Boaz secured the door before taking her by the upper arm and escorting her down the street at a brisk pace. They came upon the main market square that was still full of people who were closing up shops or buying the last-minute items before heading home.

Pausing just for a moment, Jessica bent over, hands on her knees, trying to catch her breath, the relief was short. Boaz urged her to move again, the pace even brisker than before if that was possible. They pushed through crowds of people and hurried down the street. Jessica bumped into Boaz as he abruptly halted in the entrance of a dark doorway.

Boaz turned to face Jessica. "You will need to trust me."

"What?"

Boaz grabbed Jessica and pushed her back against the door. Before Jessica could even protest, Boaz covered her mouth, pulled her leg up to his hip, and kissed her neck. Jessica gasped in fear and shock and not a moment too soon.

Jessica could barely see around Boaz's arm from her position, but she could make out at least two people, and one pointed at them. "There they are."

Boaz's grip on her thigh tightened as his body tensed. With his other hand, Boaz tilted Jessica head back and stared into her brown eyes. His eyes begged her to follow his lead.

His words echoed in her head as she held his intense gaze. She had no reason not to trust him, so she wasn't sure why a tear rolled down her cheek.

He pressed his body tighter against her, his fingers caressing her breast. She let out another gasp, glancing at the two men in the street.

The other stranger rolled his eyes at his companion. “Sure, they are.”

The man who spoke first moved toward the couple; however, he froze by the other man's words. "Leave them. They’re not the ones we are searching for."

The first man stopped. "What are you talking about? Are they not the ones?"

"You weren't paying attention to the boss, or else you wouldn't be concerned about the lovers. Let's go. We lost them plain and simple."

The two men turned around and headed back the way they came. After they were out of sight and earshot, Jessica shoved Boaz away and took off running through the streets like a startled deer. She stumbled to a halt at the entrance of an alleyway after what felt like hours.

She collapsed to the ground, her fingers digging into the dirt in front of her. She heard Boaz calling her name and paid him no mind, though she offered no resistance when he picked her up and cradle carried her down the street.

The journey back blurred in her mind, and before she knew it, they were in front of his father's house. She felt her body being shifted in his arms, just enough for him to open the door and step inside. The door shut behind them as she felt him kick it. The next thing she knew, he lowered her gently to her feet, but she kept her head ducked down.

The sound of Elchanan's voice forced her to look up, and she saw him standing in the doorway that led into the dining room. "Good, you found her. Come and eat. I fixed a light snack for dinner tonight."

She watched him turn and walk back into the room. The slight pressure of Boaz's hand on her lower back had them both moving after the older man into the dining room where they sat down. The plates on the table held pieces of different fruit and cheese with a dinner roll and cups of tea for each. Jessica sat down and picked at her food. She wasn't hungry, but she did nibble on pieces of fruit. The men's voices drifted in and out of her hearing, but her eyes sparkled with anger as Boaz started to mention the incident. She jerked her head up to glare at him, her body trembling.

"You had no right to do that." Jessica pushed her chair back and stood up. "There could've been another way."

Boaz looked at her. His face showed no anger, and in a stern voice, he said, "Pray, tell me, what other options were there? They were nearly upon us. I will not apologize for keeping you and myself safe."

Jessica gnashed her teeth together. She knocked her chair over as she ran from the room and up the stairs. Jessica went to her old room of Curator Stern's house, her body still shaking. She kicked off her shoes, crawled into bed, and turned on the lamp, and trimmed it. Jessica sank into the mattress with her back against the headboard as she angrily wiped the tears away. Snatching the Bible from the nightstand, she yanked the book open to a random page. Her eyes fell upon Jonah 4:4.

"Is it right for you to be angry about this?"

Jessica slammed the book shut, staring straight ahead. "Of course, it is," she hissed. "He's...he's so frustrating and arrogant. Not to mention pig-headed and presumptuous."

In the stillness of the room, she thought she heard a reply. "Boaz doesn't know."

She ripped open the Bible again to a random page. 'The Lord replied, "Is it right for you to be angry about this?"

Anger continued to course through Jessica's body, even though hopelessness crept into her thoughts. "He won't either. He probably thinks I'm spoiled and selfish." She sighed. "Maybe I am."

“Stop being angry. Turn from your rage.”

Jessica growled and flipped to a different page, tearing the paper in the process.

“If you forgive those who sin against you, your heavenly Father will forgive you. But if you refuse to forgive others, your Father will not forgive your sins.”

Jessica’s shoulders dropped as the anger vanished. She set the book aside and pulled her legs up to her chest. Wrapping her arms around her legs, she stared into the darkness, contemplating through the night.

CHAPTER TEN

Jessica bolted upright as sunlight passed over her face. She blinked, confused when she realized she was alone, and the night had faded. Jessica ran a hand over her face and regained her composure before stretching and getting out of bed.

Jessica didn't want to face anyone from the night before. Going over to the dresser, where she kept some of her clothes, Jessica pulled out a floor-length dress that was a lovely wine-colored shade of red. Lastly, Jessica grabbed some everyday lingerie. She set the clothing on the bed before deciding to run a bath and stall having to see anyone.

Jessica filled the claw tub up with warm water and removed her clothes, stepping inside and slowly sinking with her head resting back as she closed her eyes. The water relaxed and soothed her muscles. She bit her lip thoughtfully as she soon realized she would have to seek out Boaz's forgiveness.

It had taken Jessica most of the night to wrestle with anger and the truth that spoke to her. Even now she wasn't sure if the path she was about to choose would be correct. It would mean humbling herself before the warrior and Jessica wasn't sure if she could.

Jessica noticed the water going cool. Water splashed over the edge as grabbed the shampoo and soap, which both smelled like jasmine. It didn't take her long to finish the rest of her bathing routine.

Grabbing the bath sheet hanging nearby, she wrapped herself in it. Jessica proceeded to dry herself off and dressed. From there, Jessica went back to the chest of drawers and grabbed the hairbrush. Once the painful task of getting the tangles out of her wet hair was completed, she moved her hair off to the side and braided it, using a ribbon to tie it off. She slipped into the flats she wore yesterday before exiting her room and walked down the hall, her free hand trailing behind on the wall as she went.

Jessica made her way through the quiet house and stepped into the kitchen. She brewed herself some green tea with a hint of sugar and took a corn muffin left from last night. She warmed it up and spread some butter across the top and sat down on a stool at the counter. A folded piece of paper caught her attention. She picked up the letter.

Miss McKinney,

I'm writing to you around nine this morning. Boaz and I will be out of the house, so I want you to take the day for yourself.

Jessica smiled at Elchanan's words. She put the note on the counter, thinking of what to do next. She knew her brother was coming in to see her and Leslie. Perhaps a special dinner was in order. With that thought in mind, she stood and quickly grabbed a basket by the door, and out the door, she went.

As Jessica reached the market square, the first thing she did was step into a store. Her eyes slowly adjusted to the dim light, and as she looked around until her eyes landed on the worker, who was waiting on someone else. Stepping off to the side Jessica grabbed the fountain pen and paper and wrote down what she needed for dinner. She glanced up when she felt eyes on her. The man smiled, "Welcome to my store, my name is Anis. May I be of service?

Jessica smiled timidly back, "I need the items on this list if you have them." He took the paper and nodded his head. Grabbed a basket and his cigar and walked into the rows of food.

Jessica grew uncomfortable as the minutes ticked by, and Anis walked past her behind the counter. Jessica wrinkled her nose in disgust at the smell of the cigar. She watched as Anis added everything up, and glancing up at her said, "It will be £5, Miss." Anis's gaze never left her face. Jessica quickly fished out the money handed it over, put the items in her basket with a brisk, "Thank you." She turned and dashed out the door quickly and onto the street.

Taking a deep breath calmed her nerves. Just as quickly as she settled them, Jessica jumped back as she turned towards the street. From a butcher's stall, someone shoved a lamb shank at her. "Fresh meat for the family." was a man's voice.

She shook her head, no politely as she moved away. Another older man, asked if she would be interested in some almonds. She paused and bought a small bag, thinking it would make for an excellent addition to dinner.

She came to the vendor she wanted, knowing that the couple who owned the stall took great care in handling their fish and meat. She asked for a couple of fish, watching the man begin to the skin and clean them. Jessica paid the woman and leaned against the counter to wait until her order was ready.

After about ten minutes, she heard someone politely cough behind her. Turning around, she saw the woman with the wrapped fish. She smiled and thanked them both. She went back the way she came, the items needed for dinner in her basket.

"Hello, daughter."

Jessica paused at the sound of a familiar voice. She turned around to see her father step out from behind an empty vendor stand. Frozen with fright, Jessica stood still, though everything in her body screamed to run. When he made a move to grab her, she swung her basket at him as hard as she could. It broke, shattering upon impact, as she took off running in the opposite direction.

How did he find her after all this time? In her wildest dreams, she never thought that her parents would discover her here. She pushed past an older woman, knocked over another person who had their arms loaded with linen. In her panic stated, she didn't stop. "I am terribly sorry!"

Jessica glanced behind her before dashing across the street, trying to beat a couple of horses pulling a cart.

"Are you blind?" the driver shouted as the horses reared in surprise.

She shrugged off his words and kept running for what seemed like forever. Jessica darted down as many alleyways and different directions as she could in attempts to lose her father. She hunched over in the shadows, gasping for air. Jessica didn't see Matthew anywhere in sight.

Regaining her breath, she moved out into the main street to get her bearings, realizing she was in an unfamiliar part of the market square in Desert Sun. She noticed the buildings were run-down, the vendor stalls worn and old, and foul odors drifted through the air.

Jessica had no idea how to get back home or even who to ask for help, and after seeing her father, she wasn't thinking clearly. Jessica kept walking with her head down, and as she was passing by some vendors, she heard two voices she hadn't heard in a long time, and it gave her pause and a hopeful feeling that they could have been only on vacation and it was just a chance meeting.

Jessica stayed still and listened to the two speakers, a long-suffering sob breaking forth from her lips while she wrapped her arms around her stomach.

"Mother, do you think this will be the perfect green to go with the blue for the nursery?"

"I think it will be. Let's find out how much it is and pay for it before we find your father and Joshua for dinner."

The two women moved away. Jessica caught a glimpse of her mother and sister through the stands. They looked the same as the last time she saw them. She turned, blinking as her eyes burned from tears threatening to fall. After several attempts at guessing which direction was home, Jessica Piper McKinney found herself lost and with the afternoon sun fading into sunset. Jessica began to feel to fight a rising panic and her heart hammered in her chest. With every step Jessica took her terror was mounting. In a midst of a haze Jessica grew uneasy as a man followed behind her.

Jessica ducked into the nearest crowd to see if he would continue on his way. Jessica hurried to the middle, crouching down and pretending to browse a pottery vendor's wares. When no one approached her, she ventured away from all the people, but he was there waiting.

"Do I know you, dear?" The man reached out to touch her.

She spun around and slapped his hand away. "No."

Jessica darted across the street and down another road and into a store. The door slammed shut behind her, which turned several heads, but she didn't care. She moved away from the door and slid down to the floor and drawing her legs up as tears ran down her face leaving a trail behind. Her hair half falling out of the braid.

Some of the people began to murmur, and a couple of men started to move toward her, stopping when a desert warrior stepped forward. They backed away from the heavily armed man and his companions. He knelt beside Jessica, his gentle tone confirming to them all that he indeed knew her.

By this point, she was drowning in the deep end of memories that she couldn't fight that she didn't even hear the warrior call her name not once or twice but four times.

"Jessica!" He tapped her on her cheek. That roughly brought her back to the present.

Her gaze refocused as she looked at the warrior. "Boaz." She threw her arms around him, crying. He helped her to her feet, and they walked over to some large crates. Jessica sat down, trying to regain her composure.

Boaz whispered to one of the young warriors, who nodded and went to look in his saddle bag. He returned a few minutes later with a canteen. He opened it and offered it to her. She took it and gulped down almost half of the water.

Boaz took back the canteen and handed it to the same young warrior without looking. "What brings you down this far, woman?"

Jessica took a deep breath, but before she could speak, the door chime jingled. She looked over to see a man step inside. His voice sounded throughout the store.

"Have any of you seen a young lady come in here?"

Jessica looked at Boaz, begging him quietly, not to give her up. She watched as he turned his head to an older warrior. The warrior nodded, and she watched him move to the front. "None of us have seen a young lady entering the shop."

Jessica's ears picked up a low mumble of agreement from the body of people who were shopping in the store, and they went about their business. The man scowled and left without a word, the door banging behind him.

Jessica shook her head. “I can't go back. I just can't. Don't make me please.” She sat there, wringing her trembling hands as she watched Boaz motion for the young warrior again and whispered something into his ear.

The boy was a little bit older than her, she noticed. He nodded and exited through the back door. Boaz stood up and took hold of Jessica by the arm led her out the same way. Three horses stood outside, ready, and waiting.

The young warrior went to help Jessica, but he was surprised that she had managed to swing herself up onto the horse. Boaz looked on with a raised eyebrow. "What's wrong?" Jessica asked, perplexed at them both.

"You have some skills with a horse,” the young warrior said.

Jessica smiled faintly. "I have been riding since I was ten years old."

The younger warrior nodded his head and mounted his horse. Boaz did the same, and the group headed out.

During the ride, Jessica allowed herself to drift off into her thoughts as she bit her lower lip. *Was it just a coincidence her family was here; or was it something more? She couldn't deny it any longer, no matter how hard she wanted to. Her father wanted her back. He never cared about her, so why now? What would happen if she was forced to go back? Was she strong enough to face her childhood home?*

Jessica was brought out her thoughts as Boaz slowed his pace down and made a sharp turn down a street. Jessica noticed the fading sunset as the streets darken. Within a few blocks, Boaz pulled his horse to a halt in front of a house and dismounted. He motioned Jessica to follow suit. After hesitating for a brief moment, she did. He spoke quietly again to the young warrior who took the other two horses and left.

Jessica stood, watching the boy go. Knocking caught her attention, and she turned to see Boaz standing at a door. She moved beside him. They waited for what seemed like ages. Finally, the door opened, and there in front of them was a woman in her late thirties.

Jessica stared at the woman who had beautiful red hair that made her think of a warm flame, and soft green eyes that reminded her of a forest. She motioned them inside, and after they crossed the threshold, the woman leaned out and looked around abruptly before stepping back inside and closing the door. Turning around, she looked at them both for a time before speaking.

"They found you at last, girl, with some help."

"You mean my parents?"

"I'm not talking about your foolish parents, even though they have a hand in this."

"What do you mean? Who are you?"

Jessica soon realized the woman ignored her first question when she answered. "My name is Adele, and I am your aunt."

Jessica stared at the beautiful woman, blinked a couple of times, and then collapsed.

CHAPTER ELVEN

Boaz shook off his surprise and gathered Jessica's body in his arms, following Adele into the sitting room. The flames in the fireplace crackled softly, casting a dim glow across the furniture. Boaz positioned Jessica on the sofa while he noticed Adele turning on a lamp. He sat down next to the young girl, watching Adele hurry from the room only to return moments later with a tea tray.

"I know what you will ask. I will wait till Jessica awakes, but there is another matter, I wish to speak to you about, Jessica's fate is uncertain."

Boaz opened his mouth to speak, but Adele held up her hand to hush him again.

He took the silent hint from Adele and respectfully let her explain herself.

Adele cleared her throat and took a sip of tea. "There is a bloodline known as the O' Willow's. The O' Willow line is a royal bloodline, one that is both blessed and cursed from within. Nonetheless, there is a danger from the outside as well."

"Threats?" Boaz frowned. He was in no mood for a history lesson.

"Most of the threats are of minor importance at this moment. The threat I wish to speak of comes in the form of a group who calls themselves the Order of Keiran, or Order of the Dark. They believe that they are also descendants from the line of the O' Willow; if it's true or not, I do not know. But this group has haunted and hunted the line of the O' Willow for generations."

Boaz raised the teacup to his lips. "Why is this affair you speak of a concern?"

Adele leaned forward. "Jessica and I belong to the O'Willow line."

"Wouldn't it be patriarchal?" Boaz drank half the cup to keep the annoyance from his tone. There were more pressing matters at hand.

"No, for the line itself is a matriarch line. Unheard of in most society." Adele poured herself more tea.

Boaz raised an eyebrow. "What about if the firstborn is a male?"

"Never in the history of the royal line has a male ruled and never can. It is why the line has remained unbroken. The royal line is usually passed on from mother to eldest daughter.

Since my sister had but one male child.

"So why didn't fall to him?"

"Because my sister's firstborn was a girl who didn't make it past her first year. At any rate, Jessica's oldest sister should have been chosen. However, Ailene saw something in her youngest grandchild and made her the next Favored One."

"The Favored One?" Boaz set his cup down.

"It's the title that is held by to the next in line, and she has the mark."

Boaz glanced over at Jessica. "Marked, how?"

"An heirloom that she is supposed to wear at all times."

"How is her fate uncertain then?" Boaz asked. His frustration melted into concern. *If what Adele said was right, the plan for Jessica just became more difficult.*

Adele let out a deep breath gently as she gathered her thoughts to put them into words. "Never before has the line passed as it did. There were instances in the past that some Queens tried to. Yet, the power of line has rejected all with drastic consequences. But Jessica is different, for the power of our bloodline accepted Jessica. My sister then proceeded to make Jessica her daughter, though the child doesn't know nor her parents.

"What that could mean in the future, I do not know. Why the line accepted Jessica, I don't know."

Boaz nodded his head in thought. He turned his head slightly to where he placed Jessica and noticed a small movement from her but nothing more. He returned his focus to Adele.

~~~

Jessica blinked a few times and closed her eyes again as she heard the woman's voice. "She will need your help, Boaz, and the strength that not only runs through your veins but of our people too. I am asking you not only as of the future chieftain but as a warrior, to put aside your differences."

Jessica's face drained of color; her jaw slacked as her thoughts raced. The man she thought horribly of, maybe just maybe, wasn't who she thought he was. If he could do what this woman who claimed to be her aunt asked of him, perhaps she could too. She knew indeed she owed him an apology even more so now than before. It was here that she prayed to the Lord for forgiveness and direction not only for herself but for Boaz too.
~~~

The sound of Boaz's voice broke her thoughts, "I will do as you ask; however, I will not make a promise or a vow."

"I don't expect you to." Adele leaned forward and picked up her cup. "For you know the power of words and consequences that they hold." She proceeded to take a sip of tea.

Jessica stretched and slowly sat up before more words could be said.

Jessica felt Adele's eyes shift to her, "I have much to discuss and things to see, and little time to do so."

Jessica looked over at the woman who claimed to be her aunt. Adele stood and moved to a bookcase, where she and removed a brown leather-bound book. She moved back to the sofa where Jessica was and sat down. She proceeded to open the cover of the book, and Jessica realized it was a picture album. The first page held a picture of an elderly couple.

"These are your great-grandparents. Your great grandfather was born in 1743.

Your great grandmother was born in 1746. Your great grandmother gave birth to your grandmother in the year 1763; she was seventeen at the time." She turned the page there was a young woman, and a man beside her in her arms was a baby.

"Your grandmother had difficulties bringing young-lings into this world; it wasn't until she was twenty-seven, she gave birth to your father in 1790. He was her only child. Her passing deeply saddened me in September of 1826."

Jessica blinked back tears as Adele continued, turning to the next page. There was an older version of her grandmother and a young woman beside her. Seeing them together, she recognized the family resemblances between them. She knew then that Adele spoke the truth to her.

Adele's voice broke through her thoughts as she continued. "I was a surprise to my parents when, at the age of fifty our mother gave birth to me in August of 1796, which is unheard of. I was deemed a miracle by the doctor, so I was informed later on. Anyway, in the summer of 1814, I was eighteen when I had permission from our parents to leave for London.

“I was not happy in our homeland. For two years, I worked hard as a baker to make a living for myself as well as attending to different functions that were held at times for young ladies. It was at one of these functions I met your uncle, Jamal.

"I had worked long, and I mean long hours up to that fateful night to be able to get a perfect dress, and I bought it and shoes to go with it. But I was shunned by all of the young ladies for being different and strange to them. Do you want to know a secret?"

"What was it?" Whispered Jessica.

"I believe they were just jealous and afraid."

"Jealous and afraid?"

Adele's voice went solemn, "They are afraid since our people are still strangers and aliens to most of society. Since we are a clan, we speak an entirely different language that is still harsh sounding to many outsiders. I pray that you will never experience what I went through."

Too late. Thought Jessica as she continued to listen to the older woman and pushed her thoughts away. "What happened?"

"Jamal entered the ball that night, I had no idea he had an eye on me for a time till later, but that night he had turned many young ladies' heads. He had no eyes for them but approached me where I was sitting by myself in a corner. He didn't speak but held out his hand. I took it, and it was something I have never regretted."

"A year later, I went back home and sought out the blessing from my parents and sister, which was granted and left with him. His home and people became my home and people in return. Within that year, your great-grandparents passed away within hours of each other."

Adele closed the album and stood, walked over to the shelf, and put the book away. She motioned for Jessica to follow her. They walked up the staircase to the second floor. Pausing a few feet from the landing, Adele opened a door on the right and walked into the room.

Adele lit a wall lamp and walked over to the only piece of furniture in the room beside a box. With one graceful tug, the sheet came off of the furniture. Turning around, she folded the sheet and moved out of the way, and Jessica's eyes widening in disbelief.

Sitting there was a chest she had not seen since she was nine years old. She slowly moved forward as if in a daze. Sure enough, it was the same chest; she could tell by the carvings and latches. She knelt and front of the chest and closed her eyes, crying for the woman who loved her more than life itself. The time spent under her care was cut short, and she always wondered how different her life would have been if she could have remained with her grandmother.

CHAPTER TWELVE

Adele motioned Boaz to follow her out of the room and down the steps. When they reached the bottom, he spoke. "Does my father know?"

"He does."

"Why wasn't I informed? Especially since I had to do a search and find mission."

Adele opened her mouth to speak but paused as she glanced toward the front hall. A grim expression settled on her face and determination flashed in her eyes as she turned to Boaz. "Go back up the stairs to the room. Move to the left side of the wall and at the bottom, there is a lever that is blended in. Push on it a door will open."

Adele took a deep breath and kept talking, "Take the girl, the chest, and the box that is next to it. Be careful there is a slope, and you will move down there and stay put. There is no way out, but they shouldn't be able to find you, help will come."

Boaz opened his mouth to speak. Adele placed her fingers on his lips, "There is no time to explain, just do it, son of my heart. Go!"

She shoved him toward the stairs. He did not argue just turned and sprinted up the stairs.

Adele watched him sprint up the stairs before twirling around and hurrying into the sitting room. She moved to the far wall, and pulling down a sword, walked to the entryway, and stood ready. She didn't have to wait long, for a few seconds later the front door was kicked open. In stepped a tall man with dark brown hair and cold gray eyes.

"Get out of this house."

"Where is the Favored One?"

"Is that a new style of dress?" was her response back.

"You very well know what I am talking about."

"Do I?"

She blocked his thrust and was grateful that Jamal taught her how to handle a sword and to defend herself. Adele led Adelram through the room. As they fought, a small table with the tea set was knocked over and shattered. She managed in time to put the sofa between them and took a deep breath. With a slight glaze in her eyes almost like a soft whisp of smoke in the air before returning to normal that Adelram missed. As he came upon her, she inhaled deeply to keep her fear at bay. She looked at him with a determination of steel.

She led him back into the sitting room, thrusting, parrying, and blocking. She managed to put furniture in between them at times to slow him down.

Adele faked a miscalculation and allowed herself to be cornered. She took a deep breath, knowing her fate was sealed, as she looked at him steadily.

His left arm was bleeding slightly, and he toyed with his sword in his right hand. "You have hidden well. I thought you were just a rumor, a myth."

"What are you talking about?"

"Don't play coy with me. I know you are the ruling queen until the princess herself can come into her heritage."

Adele made a face at the man and responded, "I know of you, Adelram, and you will not get what you seek."

His smile was pure evil, "Oh, I will, and I will start with you."

Adele sensed someone come up beside her before she could turn to see who it was, a massive blow landed on the side of her head, and blackness claimed her.

~~~

Adelram looked down upon the unconscious woman for a time. Finally, he glanced at the man and spoke. "Take her out and have the men search the house." The
~~~

man nodded his head, picked up the woman, hefted her over his shoulder, and both left the house.

CHAPTER THIRTEEN

Jessica looked up as Boaz sprinted back into the room. She wiped at the tears on her cheeks, her eyes darting about in confusion when he went straight to the left wall. A gasp escaped her lips when he stepped back. She staggered to her feet at the grinding of gears and the wall moving to reveal an opening. She stood still as the warrior dragged the chest into the doorway. He motioned for her to follow, but her limbs remained frozen.

Boaz grabbed her upper arm and pushed her into the tunnel. Jessica stumbled forward, blindly groping about in the darkness. She scraped her knuckles against the wooden walls and clung to it for stability. *What was going on?*

Turning around, she saw Boaz's outline before the wall slid back into place. But as she opened her mouth to speak, he moved toward her.

"Careful now, we're moving down a slope," Boaz said. "Take your time. I'll take the chest and the box to the room below and find us a light."

A faint breeze ruffled her clothing as she felt him move past her. And the sound of something substantial being shoved down. For a time, Jessica stood in silence, then slowly shuffled along, keeping her hand on the wall as she went. Her eyes adjusted to the dark by the time she was halfway down the slope, enough to see Boaz set the box down on the chest and feel his way around the room in search of light.

The soft hiss of a match echoed in the tunnel. Jessica squinted as the lantern's light flooded the tunnel. Not a second after she'd reached the bottom. Loud noises were heard from above as if a storm were tearing the house apart.

Boaz stood stiffly by the entrance as he stared up the tunnel.

Jessica's confusion turned into fear. "What is going on? Where is Adele?"

The warrior remained still, his back to Jessica. "Adele stayed behind."

"What do you mean she stayed behind? Stayed behind for what?" Jessica's voice rose to a shriek. Before she could blink, her back collided with the wall, Boaz's hand pressed over her mouth.

The noise above them had stopped, and faint voices could be heard coming down from the slope.

Jessica didn't protest when she saw the intensity glistening in Boaz's eyes as they both strained to hear what was going on, "Thought I heard something," a masculine speaker said, "but I guess it's nothing."

Someone else replied, but they couldn't make out the words. Footsteps echoed down the tunnel. Jessica struggled to breathe with Boaz's body tensed against hers. But minutes went by, and silence returned to the house above. How long they stood like that she didn't know, but after a time, the warrior stepped away.

Boaz shook his head. "Don't you ever think, girl? If they pressed their search just a little bit more, we would have been found out, and Adele's wish for you to stay safe would have failed."

"Well, forgive me for not knowing." Jessica took a step forward, a scowl on her face. "It's not like I can read minds."

Boaz raised an eyebrow, arms crossed. "What did you think was going on?"

Jessica felt the hot burn of tears sliding down her cheeks at his stern tone.

"You need to grow up, Miss McKinney." Boaz picked up the lantern. "And stop being so childish."

Jessica glared at him through the tears. "Don't you dare tell me how to act. Don't you dare tell me what to do. You know next to nothing about me, you arrogant and pig-headed man!"

"You presume too much, child." He sat down by the chest.

"I am not a child!"

"Then prove it."

"I have to prove nothing to you, Boaz Stern!"

Boaz looked up at her, the firelight casting shadows across his face. His eyes studied her face. "Why do we always do this?"

Jessica fumbled for an answer.

He rephrased his question. "Why do we always find a reason to fight?"

Jessica opened her mouth and closed it again. She couldn't hold his gaze and glanced down, taking a deep breath as her anger subsided. "I don't know. I guess it started that night you found me."

Boaz patted the ground next to him. He remained silent until she finally accepted his invitation. "The desert life is a hard and cruel one at times. It has many hidden dangers. We who live in the desert learn quickly and grow up faster than most of society. My people are first and foremost warriors, but we are also protectors. I should have handled your situation better than I did. I was asked to find you by Adele, and take you to my father."

Jessica for the first time since their first, and with the words of her aunt and what Boaz, just said made her truly take him in thought. *The arrogance she saw maybe was from the confidence of being a leader. Did she even give a chance after that first time of seeing him?* Swallowing hard. *No. That painful word pulled from her soul and spirit and all her haste of not wanting to be under control to the point of her being powerless made her lash out more than once.* She glanced at the powerful form beside her as her eyes analyze him. Her mind analyzes their past, *He has to be a warrior, and make decisions that not only for himself but for others. If what Adele is says is true then he is next to be a king so to speak to his people. With that being said, maybe he isn't as arrogant and has compassion. He went out of his way a few times for my sake and I flung everything back in his face and yet he still tries. Am I the one at fault? Afterall?*

Jessica broke from her thoughts and looked at the handsome man clearly for the first time in the short couple of years she known, her eyes trailed over him once before flickering back up to his face before resting her eyes again on the floor. Jessica bit her lower lip. S*he knew the little bit he offered his life to her was an extended olive branch. How much should she give in return? Her past wasn't simple. Or easy to talk about and still she couldn't just speak. She weighed her choices and didn't like the outcome of any of them. However, she wasn't one to back down even when she was scared, and it took a while to work up the courage, but Jessica prayed if she opened a door that it didn't overtake her.*

"I don't even know where to begin," she whispered.

Boaz flashed her an encouraging smile. "I find the beginning always helps."

Her laughter came out more bitter than intended. "Easier said than done."

"Take your time. We should wait here for a while longer to be safe."

Jessica pulled her legs up to her chest and wrapped her arms around them. "I guess I could start with my grandmother. I lived with her for a time. She took me from my parents for reasons I don't know. I later found out it was due to my mother's secret heritage that showed up in me, and my parents resent me for it. All I know is that I have Indian blood from the Americas, and I am Irish.

"Anyway, I was eight years old when things began to change. It was my birthday. I remember it was a beautiful but chilly afternoon. I had been wearing a white dress that my Grandmamma made for me. I was spinning in the window room, having fun. Grandmamma had stood watching me before she left. Sometime later, a maid came in and told me the guests were arriving. My sister was throwing a fit for it wasn't about her.

"After the party, Grandmamma called me to her side and clasped a beautiful cross necklace around my neck with a warm smile. She told me I was her princess, her Favored One. And to this day, I hadn't taken it off for fear of losing it like the one day when it nearly got knocked down the drain. I started to take lessons from Grandmamma on how to act and not act as people do in snobbish society."

Boaz raised an eyebrow. Jessica took a deep breath at his look. "But my happy life with Grandmamma didn't last. Grandmamma mysteriously became ill barely a year into my lessons, and a couple of days later, she passed away. I was placed back with my parents, and Aine came with me. It was after the funeral that I overheard my sister talking to our father about the chest of clothes that was a gift to me from Grandmamma. She told him she would benefit from them more than I. And our father agreed.

"The next day, the chest and some of our grandmother's things disappeared, and no one could find them. At first, my sister tried to accuse me, and it was the only time our mother stood up for me because I wouldn't have been able to move it.

"It was during this time that I slowly realized my family other than Aine didn't love me, and later David and a few servants.

How was I supposed to understand that when someone shows interest or asks things of you that they don't always do with care and love? I learned that lesson the hard way."

Boaz put a reassuring hand on her shoulder. "There's no shame in wanting to see the good in people."

Jessica tried to smile, but judging by the flicker of concern in Boaz's eyes, she was sure it looked more like a grimace. "I have a hard time believing that after what happened."

Boaz squeezed her shoulder. "There's no need to continue if you are uncomfortable."

Jessica looked down, wringing her hands together. *She felt safe with him, yet did he need to know so much about her?* She glanced up at him. Seeing the concern in his face gave her the courage to continue, and with a deep breath, she said, "A friend of my father took an interest in me, and he called it playing house. He would take me behind our house or into a room when no one else was around. He would touch me. I remember one time I had to touch him, and I remember it so well because I could see my mother from where we were. I prayed she would turn around, but she never did.

"It wasn't until later that a couple of his friends joined him. One taught me how to touch myself, and another showed me what he wanted me to do with a demonstration. Some would kiss me, touch me, or rub their bodies again. Then one of them got naked and held me on top of him and forced me to rub myself against him."

Jessica's voice trembled, and her body shook. "Even now, those sensations come back to haunt me, and I hate them. I wish they would go away!"

Boaz wrapped his arms around her. He whispered words of comfort in his mother tongue. "You are stronger than you know, dear one. You don't have to relive nightmares anymore."

She cried as she clung to him. She fought to regain her composure and pulled away from him, wiping her nose and eyes on her sleeve. "I have to. I started, and I need to finish."

"Then, I will listen."

Jessica shifted away, sitting up straight and clearing her throat. "At one point, David walked into one of those sessions and put a stop to it. I wasn't left alone ever again. But David and Aine pretended nothing happened and tried to move on from it. There's more that they don't know, and it haunts me to this day."

She stood and started to pace as she spoke, "I was picked on and teased by my sister and her friends. I remember one day I was shoved down, and one of her friends tore my upper part of my dress and said I was ugly. Another came at me with a knife after finding out that someone she fancied had helped me and almost stabbed me in the back, she did manage to slice my left upper thigh. I was also punched and choked and pushed down the stairs three different times and hit my head."

"My parents weren't much better. They often ignored me, but the servants made sure I had what I needed. I worked alongside them when I could to show my gratitude. Then one day, my parents found out about me playing with some common children that belonged to a friend of Aine's. Father was going to fire Aine, but I told him it was my idea and not hers and that she didn't know.

“Father beat me until I passed out. I remember being sick for days afterward, for father had locked my room, and no one could come in to check on me. When Aine was able, it was almost too late, and it took her a few months to get me healthy again."

The light sputtered as if a breeze disturbed the flame. Boaz held up a hand, looking toward the tunnel, and slowly searched the room. But the lantern's fire returned to normal, and he motioned for her to continue.

"My sixteenth birthday was the last event that sent me on my way to you. I worked hard, designing the perfect dress for it. I knew my parents would not celebrate, but I also knew they would throw a party not to make themselves look bad in the eyes of the community or the clan.

“I was asked by Joshua, one of the most attractive boys if he could escort me to the party. I said yes. I foolishly thought that maybe my life was starting to get better.

"Aine and a couple of the maids saved up enough money for the materials I needed for the dress. A friend of Aine's was kind enough to let me have a pair of shoes to go with it after she saw the finished dress. I had bathed and soaked for hours that day. A maid helped rub scented oils into my skin and twisted my hair into an elegant bun. She even brushed enough color to highlight my cheeks and eyes.

"As a dutiful daughter, I started to greet the guests, being polite to each, and moving on. It hurt knowing the whispers that followed me, but I ignored them that night for my mind was set on finding Joshua. But I heard his voice once I reached the balcony. I moved closer to the balcony doors, and I opened them slightly to listen in on his conversation.

“I heard my sister say, “Why did you ask her and not me? I thought you fancied me?”

“Oh, but I do, Rebecca, dearest,” he said.

“Then tell me so I can understand.”

"I was dared to take Jessica to bed. Just for one night. To see what it would be like with a lowly maiden."

"I still don't understand why you want to do that. There is nothing extraordinary about my sister. Just plain and ugly."

"Now, now, no pouting, my love. For it is you I wish to marry. I was planning on asking for your hand very soon."

“I had heard all I could stand and stepped onto the balcony. “You both deserve each other then. How could I be so blind? I should have known better!” I turned around to leave, but not before I heard Rebecca say that I was a disgrace to the family.

"I was headed toward the food table to distract myself when I felt someone push me, and I tripped over the skirt of my dress and fell right onto the table. I heard the cruel taunting from some of my peers and a few from the older guests. I heard horrifying gasps from others as I was struggling to get myself up and to stand when a shadow fell over me. I turned and saw my father standing over me.

"His words were like ice. "How can you embarrass me like this? Get up and go to your room."

"As I stood, I locked eyes with my mother with hope. But she turned and walked away, and it was at that moment I realized there was no love for me, and nothing I could do would ever win that love. I ran from the ballroom and up the staircase and collapsed on them. Aine found me, and before I knew it, I was packed into a buggy, then onto a ship, and found myself on a terribly long travel route until I came to Cairo. I suppose you know the rest."

Jessica couldn't keep her composure. Boaz stood upon the fading of her words and moved to her. He gently pulled her to him. She clung to him again, crying, and whispered, "There is so much."

Boaz didn't respond to Jessica, but pulled her closer, as he guided her over to the chest and sat down upon it. He sat her on his lap and she buried her face between his neck and shoulder. After a small amount of time, he spoke. "You did not deserve any of that to happen. It isn't your fault, woman. None of it is."

"I just want these memories to go away! Please!" She begged.

He closed his eyes and *thought women were meant to be treasured and to be loved, cherished, respected, protected for they gave life.* His arms tightened around her. "I can't make them go away, Jessica. Those things should never have been done to you. It's your body's way of responding to something natural, even if you didn't like it."

She cried harder than before.

~~~
~~~

All Boaz could do was hold Jessica and kiss her softly on the temple and whisper soothing words to her. *If she had been among his people, and the abuse had happened, the individuals involved would have died without hesitation. The child or woman would have gotten the help they needed.*

Jessica's crying eventually stopped, and she fell asleep in his arms. The warrior himself was still awake, keeping watch not only on the surroundings but on the sleeping girl. *No*, he thought, *she is a woman, hurt and scared and so much like a child.* A noise broke Boaz's train of thought, and he stood up. Jessica awoke at this sudden movement that had her back on her feet.

They both looked at the wall where the scraping noise came from. Boaz removed a dagger from his person, gave it to her, and pointed to the other side of the room. She moved with no questions asked. Boaz lifted his sword, waiting.

The wall to the right of the chest seemed to be pulling back, and the next sound heard was two blades hitting each other and echoing through the room. The warrior who stepped in had the same black clothes on like Boaz.

Boaz replaced his weapon as he recognized his kinsman. They greeted each other and moved aside for the rest of the group to enter. Four of them were warriors of their village who bowed to Boaz in the way of greeting and stepped aside by the entrance to wait. Four others came in after, two men and two women. With that, he shifted his stance so that he could keep an eye on his charge as the four moved slowly into the room.

Boaz attention turned back to his kinsman as they spoke in low tones. Boaz attention turned back to his kinsman as they spoke in low tones. Boaz noticed Jessica's movement toward the chest, where she stood in front of it as he listened to the other warrior.

It was Jessica shout, "No! I don't care. I told you no!" that made Boaz completely turn and took on the situation more carefully. He motioned to his warriors by the door and spoke a soft command to them.

Boaz watched as they approached carefully. The girl's eyes met his for a moment, and he nodded his head.

He watched as she bit her lip and slowly stepped aside as the two warriors moved. One placed the box on the chest and, bending down, they picked the chest up and carried it with them to the entrance.

Jessica immediately moved to him. When she reached him, he took the dagger from her and sheathed it. Boaz then introduced her to the other warrior, who had beautiful grey-blue eyes and dark brown hair. His face seemed familiar from the slope of his nose to the arch of his eyebrows, the shape of his eyes and high cheek bones. Overall, he was very handsome. He was nearly as tall as Boaz and the air about him exuded authority and protection. He seemed to be very aware of his surroundings and serious yet warm. With all the command of his presence, his eyes showed caring.

"Jessica, this in Kontar," Boaz said calmly.

He watched her movements silently as she held out her hand and said, "It's nice to meet you."

His eyes sparkled with mirth as his friend kissed the back of her hand and said, "The pleasure is mine."

Jessica reacted to his kiss as if she'd put her hand into a boiling pot of water. She pulled her hand back quickly and stepped closer to Boaz. He noticed but acted naturally instead. "Shall we move out?"

"Yes," she responded in agreement. They exited the room, moved down the tunnel, and out into the late, warm evening. He inhaled deeply and noticed Jessica doing the same since she didn't leave his side. He felt Jessica turn slightly away from him as he moved to the cart. Boaz only paused when he didn't sense her following anymore.

In turning Boaz and his kin were watched the scene play. As one of the women licked her lips, her voice drifted to them as she spoke. "We are a part of the clan. We were there when your grandmother gave you the necklace, and we are here to help-."

Jessica interrupted the other woman. "Here to help me? That is a joke. Where were you when Grandmamma took on a mysterious illness? Where were you when I suffered from the hands of my so-called family and their friends? Were you there?"

Jessica paused to catch her breath and continued in a shrill and deafening voice. "No, you were not; you were nowhere to be seen! Now you come out of the blue and claim you want to help me? That you are part of my family clan? I don't think so, and you have no right to that. You had your chance, and you all missed it! Stay away from me!"

~~~

Boaz was ready for the girl who barreled into him sobbing. He wrapped his arms around her and did not say a word. He noticed one of the men went to object but stopped as he let his displeasure and anger show on his face. He slowly bent his head
~~~

and whispered, "Get into the front of the cart."

She nodded her head, and he helped her climb into the front of the cart. He jumped in next, and Kontar took the reins from him as he climbed in from the other side. He looked behind him to see the others in the cart. His warriors sat by the chest, and the other four sat sullenly he noticed at the end of the wagon. Turning back around, he gave the quiet signal, and Kontar flicked the reins, and they began making their way through the quiet streets.

In about an hour, Kontar pulled the reins, and the cart and horses came to a halt. Boaz and two of the other warriors jumped down first. Boaz pulled Jessica down and into his arms. As he turned, light from the doorway, shone out. The door opened and standing just inside of the entryway was a young woman in her mid-twenties. She was slightly overweight with warm and bright hazel eyes and chocolate brown hair. Her voice was like a breeze; gentle and light as she spoke.

"Was she harmed?'

There was a significant concern in her eyes for her young friend, and it showed. A man from Jessica's clan spoke with a slow and somewhat heavy accented voice. "Why does it matter to you?"

Michele forgot protocol entirely. "It is my concern since she is a dear friend of mine. Why don't you leave off!"

Before any of the four could respond, Kontar spoke sharply. "Enough, Michele. Leave us, woman."

~~~

The woman bit her lip. Spinning around; she went back inside the kitchen where she resumed her task of dicing up tomatoes roughly at the counter. Her thoughts drifted to the day she first met Jessica. *They met quite by accident when Jessica found herself turned around in the market.*

The lost look on Jessica's face moved her, and a few women who had rare permission to come to the city. They helped her immediately. They took a
~~~

liking to the shy and quiet girl who was talkative and funny when the mood struck her. She worried they would never be close as friends, but cared for the younger girl nonetheless.

Lost in her thoughts, she didn't hear the order from Boaz. "Carry the girl's belongings upstairs and guard them."

Michele never heard the warriors come through with the hope chest and box as they moved through the kitchen.

CHAPTER FOURTEEN

A tense moment passed by before Boaz moved into the house closely followed by Kontar, and then the others followed behind. They walked through the kitchen and into the dining room where a group of people sat around the table. The four outsiders stopped and took up seats after they realized that they were immediately blocked from the stairs by two guards who stood watch by the doorway.

Taking a sharp left up the stairs and into the girl's room, Boaz lay Jessica on the bed. Turning around, he started to walk back to the doorway where Kontar waited. His movements were stilled by a touch. Looking behind him, he saw Jessica was awake with sleep-heavy eyes as she stared at him. Her tired voice spoke, "Stay."

"I cannot."

"Why?"

"It would be improper of me to do so."

"Please."

"You are in my father's house, and safe you will be. Some of our warriors will be outside guarding."

He knelt by the bed as he brought her hand up and kissed it before tucking it back into her. Boaz smoothed the hair from her forehead, and whispered, "Sleep, dear one, while you still have the chance this night."

Jessica didn't fight sleep. As she felt warm lips on her forehead she drifted off into her dreams. Boaz stood and turned to Kontar, a silent conversation between them as they made their way out of her room. Both Boaz and Kontar moved back downstairs. When they stepped back into the room Boaz realized something must have happened while they were upstairs, as they silently took in the scene.

~~~

A woman stood up, and her chair pushed back roughly. Her right hand held the hilt of an ancient sword. The sword itself was thirty-eight inches long altogether. The handle was wood with a sliver of silver from the steel showing on the sides.

Engraved into the wood in gold was a strange symbol. The blade had vines on one side of the sword, and in some places woven between runes on the opposite side. Both sides of the sword mirrored one another.

She had slammed this sword into the middle of the table. The runes seemed to glow just a little. Her stature grew, and the woman's eyes held a fire of anger that burned from within. The air in the room seemed to take on a dense and heavy feeling. By this point, she narrowed her eyes as she felt the next in line to be the protector. She kept that to herself for it wasn't time to
~~~

reveal them. For their safety and protection, as well as Jessica's, they needed to remain hidden.

As she let go of the sword, she slammed her hands onto the table, responding to the other woman. "Don't you dare! If it weren't for the clan's meddling, we wouldn't have this crisis, to begin with!"

"We did what we needed to do to keep the royal line safe!"

"No, Priscilla, ye all did it so the heiress would be kept ignorant!"

"She was bereaved!"

"Don't justify your reckless behavior by preying on a young girl's grief."

"Well, you need to start looking beyond just your opinion on the matter."

"No, I should have never let my grief consume me. It will no more!"

"You..." Priscilla's voice trailed off.

The woman said, "Excuse me, Priscilla, ye are as thick as manure but not as useful!"

Everyone waited with baited breath as the woman's words slowly dawned on Priscilla, and her eyes narrowed with hateful anger. "Why you little..."

"Enough!" A wise old voice spoke loudly.

All eyes turned to the end of the table, where an elderly man sat. In a softer voice, he said, "The protector is right. We interfered with not only her responsibilities, but we also interfered with the royal line which the faithful shouldn't have done. By doing so, we disrespected the last wishes of our beloved late queen and not without consequence."

Objections arose among the clan members. The elder raised his hands for silence, and slowly, the room grew quiet again. He lowered his hand and leaned forward with his hands clasped and said, "We will allow the protector to do her duties."

"He can't be serious?" whispered someone.

"Oh, I am deadly serious. You all must pray that the consequences will not be severe due to our meddling. All of you are dismissed for the evening."

He left no room to argue in his tone of voice. One by one, the clan left the house. The woman who still stood, the elder, Elchanan, Kontar, Boaz, and a couple of warriors remained behind.

Slowly the old man stood, but paused as she spoke her eyes still focused, "Would you two gentlemen watch over the girl this night."

Kontar answered as they were leaving the room, "We will."

When they did, she let out a small sigh of relief, and she reached for the sword and re-sheathed it.

"Do you have a plan?" the elder asked.

She thought a moment before looking at him, and carefully responded, "I do."

"Will it work?"

"It's not foolproof if that is what you mean."

She continued before he could speak. "What plan isn't completely without risk?"

"Be that as it may Aine, I am still concerned."

"Your concern has been noted, Brian, and dismissed. You all made a mess of things already, and I allowed it, to my shame. The plan should buy some time."

"I understand, but..."

"If that is all gentlemen, I will be retiring for the night."

Elchanan stood up as Aine moved away from the table with the sword in hand. Pausing at the doorway, she turned and looked at the chieftain. "Thank you for watching out for her as a father would do, and for opening your home to us. I deeply appreciate it."

She left the room and went up the stairs, pausing at the door that held her charge. The four warriors watched over her, two on the inside and two in the hallway.

Satisfied, she moved toward her room, closing the door behind her. She placed the sword against the wall and slipped out of her dress and underclothes. She walked to the suitcase and pulled out a slip and stepped into it before getting into bed. Arms wrapped around her and a male body pressed close.

"How'd it go?" a soft, thick, masculine voice asked.

"Well enough to be expected. But the fight is only beginning, and it's time for the old to wane, and the new to wax as the moon does."

She rolled over, reaching up to caress his face. "Do not worry about me, my love. I know the day is coming, and I will gladly hand over the line to the one who is more worthy than I. For, I have failed in many ways."

He went to speak, and she placed one of her fingers on his lips to silence him. "I am alright with this, and ye should be too. For the one we consider as a daughter will be safe. We have a plan, even if it is shaky.

However, right now, I need my lover's comfort, David, to hold and love me this night."

He kissed her finger and said, "As you wish, my dear."

CHAPTER FIFTEEN

The night turned into fore-dawn and found the room occupants already starting their day. Aine had gone down the stairs to start breakfast, and David dismissed the tired warriors back to their people while he took a seat by Jessica's bed and waited.

It was roughly another hour when Jessica started to wake up, stretching, and blinking her eyes.

"Top of the morning to you, sunshine."

She jolted upright and saw David. She scrambled from the bed and dove at him. David barely kept the chair from tilting backward and pulled her tightly into a hug just as fiercely as she was embracing him. She pulled back and traced his face with her fingertips.

"I missed you both so much," she whispered. "Is Aine here too?"

He smiled. "Yes. Downstairs making breakfast." He squeezed her hand and stood. "I will draw a bath for you, Miss Jessica, and let you get your day started."

"You don't have to do that, David, and don't call me that, please. I haven't been your...," Jessica choked on the words,"...*mistress* for a long time."

He just smiled and turned into the bathroom and started to prepare her bath.

~~~
~~~

Jessica placed her feet on the floor and her hands on the edge of the bed and bit her lower lip thoughtfully. *She saw how he smiled at her and the change in demeanor. Jessica wondered if he didn't realize how much she missed him and what he and Aine meant to her. Maybe she would reinforce that sometime today. She would let them know how it tore her apart when she was forced to leave them behind.*

She heard the door shut, glancing up, noticed David left. She went to the dresser and pulled out fresh underclothes and an everyday dress. Nothing fancy. It had short sleeves, a square neckline, and slightly above ankle length.

Jessica rushed through her bath, having dried and dressed in under ten minutes. She pulled her wet, tangled hair back with a hair clip and ran out of the room and down the hall and stairs. Before walking into the dining room, Jessica took a few deep breaths to calm her herself.

She saw David sitting there, sipping on coffee. Beside David sat a young woman who grew up in the same household as

Jessica. They were on different ends of the spectrum in many ways. "Quinn?"

Jessica watched as the woman in question glanced up and smiled brightly at her with words, "Top of the morin' to ye, Miss Jessica."

Jessica dashed across the room and pulled Quinn up and into a hug. It was a second later that she felt Quinn's arms around her. She barely even noticed that Aine had placed two plates of breakfast down and walked away.

The two girls chattered away, catching each other up with news and gossip. Quinn asked Jessica about her life here, and Jessica began her precise answer in their home language. Quinn just smiled and nodded at the right times until Jessica came to a stop.

Quinn giggled uncontrollably, and managed to say, "You can still talk a mile a minute, and I am glad you haven't changed in that at least. As for me, I left your family's employment a few months after you left. After my mother and a few others were let go by your parents."

Jessica's eyes widened.

"It's not your fault. We all planned on leaving once you got out of there, so it's not a heartbreak."

"What do you mean?"

"Some of us only stayed for you young mistress and nothing more."

Jessica's mouth formed an O, and before she could respond to ask her more, a voice interrupted.

"I want you both to eat, and I expect that your plate to be half-eaten, young lady. You are still far too thin." Aine proceeded to hand David's plate to him and set her plate upon the table.

Jessica stared at Aine. She knew better than to talk back to her. Her mouth was washed out with soap. She was thirteen.

She couldn't remember why, but she'd thrown a tantrum and been quite obstinate. She learned her lesson with a sound spanking thrown in for good measure.

"I see I am not as important to you as I once was."

Jessica blinked and came back to the present. She rushed over to the older woman and hugged her tightly. "Yes, you are. Don't say that."

Aine returned the gesture, then stood back and looked her up and down and kept her thoughts to herself. She ushered the girl to her seat. The other two stood and waited for her to be seated, and the others did likewise. It was one of the more traditional breakfasts from home, fried tomatoes, and bread, with bacon and eggs with a cup of hot tea to wash it down.

The others hid their smiles as Jessica wrinkled her nose and pushed the bacon away. She never cared for pork, and she wasn't going to start now.

"I expect you to eat one piece of that bacon," Aine said.

Jessica whispered her response out loud. "You can't be serious?"

"Yes, I am."

Jessica looked up and frowned at her caretaker.

"Don't frown, child. It will give you wrinkles later in life."

Jessica snatched up a piece of bacon and wolfed it down, grabbing her warm tea and drinking half of it to hide the taste. She ate her food slowly, and by the time she finished half of her plate and pushed it away, the others were done eating.

David and Quinn stood up as one. "Aine, Quinn, and I will be back later to help with dinner. She wanted to explore a little, and I can pick up those few items you need to. It will give Jessica and you a chance to spend time together."

Aine nodded, and the two left.

"Have fun and stay safe," Jessica called out to them.

"Where is the fun in that?" asked Quinn, who smiled and walked out behind David.

The two women proceeded to clean up the breakfast plates and cups and worked getting the kitchen back in order. After Jessica placed the last dish away, she turned and looked at Aine.

"I wanted to let you know that I missed you both so much. Not a day has gone by that I didn't think about you both. I was so scared when you made me leave, and it hurt."

Aine placed the towel on a rack to dry and turned to look at her. "Me girl, what has brought this on?" She held out her arms to her, and Jessica ran into them, crying. "Shh... young one, we miss ye just as much, and it hurt us just as much."

Jessica nodded, gathering her composure.

"Come, there is much to talk about and little time to do so." She motioned to Jessica to grab the two glasses. She grabbed the pitcher that held fresh homemade lemonade, and they went into the sitting room and sat down. Aine poured the lemonade into the glasses, and they sipped them until the glasses were empty.

Jessica poured the second helping of the refreshing drink. Sitting back down and taking her glass, Jessica grew nervous in the quiet. She noticed something off with Aine and became uncomfortable.

CHAPTER SIXTEEN

Before Jessica could ask what was the matter, Aine spoke.

"There has been much that has been kept from ye after your grandmother's passing away. I will tell ye what I can and do my best to answer your questions. But there will be a lot that I can't. Hopefully, in the neigh future, ye will discover the answers. What I am about to speak of was supposed to be told to ye long before now, but my hands were tied. Or I should say; I allowed them to be tied in my grief, so to speak."

Jessica tried to speak again, but Aine raised her hand to silence her, "Let me finish before ye ask your questions. It will make this easier and quicker."

She nodded her head to show that she understood, and Aine proceeded again. "Yer grandmother, father, sister, and ye are part of a royal line. A royal bloodline, to be exact. Ye grandmother was the last queen. On yer eighth birthday, she placed her favor on ye and had chosen ye to be the true heiress and princess. The line is always passed down from mother to the oldest daughter. If there is no daughter, then the oldest son's daughter will get it.

"Nonetheless, whatever yer grandmother's reasoning, whatever she saw or sensed in ye, made her break with tradition and made ye the next in line to be queen. Ye know the proud history of our homeland that we were made up of many governing clans."

Aine waited as she watched Jessica nod her head before continuing. "Our clan was one of the most powerful ones, but we were the last to fall, for we were betrayed. The story that was passed down from my mother and hers and so forth was this; the ruling queen at that time placed her protector and heiress in the hidden room along with items of the house to keep them all safe. Before she and the others went out and met the enemy head-on in the battlefield.

“Only a few survived by the end of the massacre and managed to escape into the fields. Ye met a few of the faithful last night. After that time, the protector and royal bloodline went into hiding to keep the line safe, pure, and untouched. Until recently. Somehow, they found out about the lines still being around. It places you in danger, and that fills me with concern."

"Me?"

"Ye are very important, Jessica, and there will be those who wish to seek to hurt you and take control of the power you hold. The line of the protector has always been close to the royal line, for they are the last and only true defense that can keep the queen and princess safe now."

"There is more, isn't there? More you are not telling me? Who is the protector? Why me, I am nothing special, just worthless!"

"Oh, me girl yer not worthless. Yer exceptional indeed, more than you realize."

"But I am! I can't do anything, right!"

"Nonsense, yer not worthless. I had hoped the time away from that environment would help ye to see that ye are not, and put more confidence in yerself. But I was wrong, so it seems."

Aine let out a tired sigh and stared at Jessica, who had bitten her lower lip. She whispered, "Then why can't I see."

"In time ye will see, me girl."

"As for the protector, ye have known them for yer whole life."

"No, I haven't!"

"Who has always been a constant presence in yer life?"

"Well, there are some of the servants when they could, Quinn, David, and you."

The last word was spoken almost to hear softly. As Jessica thought back over her life, she realized that it was Aine who came to live in her parent's house to take care of her after grandmamma died, and none of the other servants did.

Realization washed over her as Aine smiled grimly at the young lady as she whispered, "It's you? Isn't it?"

Aine stood up and moved to kneel in front of her.

"I am the last line of the protectors, Princess of the O' Willow line. I will uphold my duties and responsibilities that have been passed down through the years. If ye will have me still."

Jessica bit her lip unsure, and said, "I accept your oath, protector."

It was enough for Aine as she stood before her future queen and young charge. She didn't get far for Jessica had hugged her around the middle of her waist and clung tightly to Aine. Aine managed to sit down beside her. There they sat for hours, half chime from the grandfather clock sounded that it was half-past one in the afternoon.

Aine stood up and said, "We need to fix at least a light lunch for us to eat." Jessica nodded and knew just the thing. Standing, they moved to the kitchen area.

Aine went to the cold room and pulled out a few things that had been prepared already. "What should we make with this? It looks it had be prepped last night; probably from that woman."

Jessica paused, looking through the cupboards. "Oh, that would save us some time. Put those on the counter, and I will show you what we will be making."

Taking out a deep bowl, she moved to where Aine stood and proceeded to show Aine how to make the salad.

She placed the diced cucumber and tomato in the dish and mixed it, then she topped it with the diced onion. Then in the smaller bowl, mixed some garlic, olive oil, and lemon juice. Next, she added salt and pepper to taste.

Jessica then took the mixture and drizzled it on the salad then topped it with chopped parsley. Then she took out two smaller dishes and dished it out into two servings on plates. They took the plates back to their room and ate in silence.

Aine set her fork down and looked at Jessica thoughtfully. Jessica felt eyes on her and looked up to find Aine studying her.

"Do you hate that I sent ye away?"

Jessica took a deep breath. *This is not the opening she wanted and needed, but the words would be hard to come by*. She let it out slowly, calming her nerves.

"I was hurt and scared, as I said before. But to hate David and you, I could never do that. For the longest time, I was mad and confused as to why you did. That is in the past, and I have forgiven you both since then."

"Do you like it here?"

Jessica placed her fork down as she responded, "It has not been bad. Taking some time to adjust, especially with the heat. I will be honest; the first part of my stay was the worst."

Aine looked down thoughtfully.

"What happened?"

"I could barely get by. Couldn't find work. It's a man's society in every sense of the word here."

"The curator?"

"I was found on a street corner in Cairo late one night in the middle of a rain shower. I was sitting there, hopeless and afraid until Boaz found me. He came over to me and picked me up when I did not respond to him. I tried running from him but he caught me, so I started to hit and kick him, but I couldn't break his hold.

"He placed me on his horse and brought me to this city, to the museum where I was introduced to the curator. The same night I found out he was his son. We can't stand each other." Jessica trailed off unsurely.

"What has changed?" Asked Aine.

"Last night." Was the girl's vague answer.

"Will ye tell me?"

"No." Speaking softly just above a whisper.

"Remember ye both grew up in different cultures, so ye will both see things differently. Communication is important, as is open honesty with each other. Ye must try to understand each other's point of view."

"What are you saying Aine?"

The older woman smiled softly.

"Ye will know when the time comes. I hope ye will with what I am about to say. 'Love is patient, love is kind. It does not envy, it does not boast, it is not proud. It is not rude, it is not self-seeking, it is not easily angered, it keeps no record of wrongs. Love does not delight in evil but rejoices with the truth. It always protects, always trusts, always hopes, always perseveres. Love never fails.' Do ye remember this scripture?"

Jessica frowned as she shook her head no.

"It's from Paul's first letter to the Corinthians. Chapter 13, verses four through eight. We also know it as the love chapter."

Jessica inhaled sharply at that as Aine stood and gathered the plates, cups, and the pitcher and left the room. A moment later, she came back in and wiped the table down. Pausing at the door, she turned and asked.

"Are ye still studying?"

"I am. I have private tutors that are hired by the curator. He thought it would be best for me to have one, as I have some difficulty focusing. If things remain the same, I will be done this year."

"How are ye coming along?"

"Average marks."

"I am happy to hear that ye continued yer studies. What will ye do next?"

"I haven't thought about that honestly. I still don't know what I would like to do."

"I see. I will leave, now me girl. If ye have a need, let me know. I have a few things I must attend to before dinner. When

David and Quinn get back, send them to me, please."

"I can do that for you," smiled Jessica. She got up and hugged Aine tightly and whispered, "I love you."

"I know, and I do love you too, my sweet."

Aine broke the embrace and left the room. Jessica sighed lightly. She moved toward the other side of the room, to the bookshelf. Selecting *Pride and Prejudice* by Jane Austen, she sat down and began to read.

An hour had gone by when David and Quinn came back with their arms laden with purchases. She sent them to Aine and offered to help them, but they quickly refused. Jessica shrugged and went back to reading. Sometime later, as she was finishing the last chapter, the sound of hurried footsteps approached her room. Brent and Leslie burst through the door, worried, and embraced her.

They demanded to know what happened. She eased their fears as much as possible by explaining the run-in with her old family and found some lovely people who brought her back to the curator's after she was lost in the lower Midbar Shemesh marketplace. She left out a lot of what happened. She had a feeling that if she didn't, it might not be a good thing. She asked Brent how long he would be here and he began to fill his little sister in on what was going on in his life.

Soon, they were interrupted by Quinn, who stated dinner was ready as they entered the dining room. Elchanan, along with David and Aine who both had just placed the last of the meal on the table. But she soon realized Boaz wasn't there, even though his father was.

It was Elchanan only who noticed the girl searching the room. Jessica frowned for she had wanted to thank Boaz. It looked like it wasn't going to happen, and then Jessica realized the meal that was on the table ready to be served was her favorite meal.

"We couldn't find Haddock fish, and I hope you don't mind having Perch," said David.

"No, it is fine, and it looks yummy," whispered Jessica.

She stared at the baked Perch that was broiled with lemon, butter, white wine, and homemade breadcrumbs and served with creamy seasoned vegetables for the side dish. She sat down, and they began eating the meal in silence. Gradually, small talk filled the air throughout dinner. When dinner was over, they ushered out the siblings into the other room with plates of fig and ginger upside-down cake. For the rest, they had to finalize the plan they would put into motion the next day. Soon the night drew on and found the house occupants retiring for the night.

CHAPTER SEVENTEEN

Before any of them realized, almost three months had passed them by and it was now the third of February of 1837. Nonetheless, it didn't make it any easier for everyone involved with the plan, especially Jessica. Jessica was worried about Quinn, who took on the role of decoy, and she took it seriously. The next day when she found out, she had thrown a fit of worry because she didn't understand why Quinn had to pretend to be her. No one gave her any logical answers, and her older siblings were just as clueless.

It had been Quinn instead of Aine who put her foot down, and she kept it down. She held to the fact that, "This is what family and friends do to help the one in trouble."

She had taken Jessica's hands and continued. "You are my best friend and one I consider a sister since we grew up together. Allow me this honor Jess to keep you safe from your family. At the very least buy us time to come up with another solution."

The morning had started as any other day, but Jessica soon realized it wasn't. For nothing had been going well from the time she left her bed to now. Even David, Aine, and Quinn seemed to be having troubles of their own before they went from the house to play their roles as a decoy, protector, and guardian.

Jessica paused and slipped her heels off. Why of all days did she wear them she wondered? It was bad enough running late getting to work because of a math assignment. She even skipped breakfast to finish it, which in turn made her late for work. Jessica was out of breath as she ran up the driveway and the steps. Before going in, she froze. Jessica saw many people through the glass doors, and she stared in shock.

Never had she seen the museum this busy, not even on the best of days. Before she could step inside, Leslie stepped out and pulled her away quickly from the doors and to the side and out of sight. Leslie began to jabber. Her voice gave away her upset state.

"Good, you are finally here! You are to go to the closed portion of the museum and unload the crates and sort them out today. Dr. Stern doesn't want you to be seen, for some reason. He is concerned and worried. He tried to put me on the assignment with you, but one of the newer workers stated they need help. Go now and quickly; but go around and come in from the back. Immediately before someone sees you! He doesn't want you to be seen, it's all so very strange to me!"

She pushed Jessica towards the steps and went back in just as quickly. Jessica turned and stared at her sister for the longest time they held each other's gazes through the doors before she turned and hurried down the steps and around the building. Taking out her keys, she unlocked the backside door and stepped inside just as a drizzle of rain began to fall. Jessica turned and locked the door.

Then she made her way down the quiet hall until she came to a closed gate, unlocked it, and stepped inside. Turning around, Jessica shut the door and let the lock click back into place. She trimmed some lights and noticed the crates had already had been opened for her, which made her job much easier.

She removed the lid on one crate, then removed the packing material carefully. She started to place the contents on the table one by one. After some time, she had everything from the first crate unloaded. She wished that her sister was here to help.

Sorting and doing the dating on the texts were not her expertise, but she would try her hardest to do it correctly. She reached for paper and a pen along with the other items she needed from one end of the table. She started to catalog the items inside the crate. Two hours into her work, Jessica paused, turning around and slowly swept her gaze across the room; a sudden noise disturbed her focus. Finding nothing abnormal, she shrugged her shoulders and went back to work. A short time later, she noticed a shadow drifted over her light.

She took in a sharp, quiet breath. The body belonging to the shadow spoke. "I see you haven't changed a bit in the least, which in and of itself is amazing."

Jessica scrambled to her feet and took a few paces back to put some space between them. Once she did, she took in the man's features and realized it was Joshua. *In some ways, she noticed he was more mature, statuesque, and athletic in build. Nonetheless, an image of Boaz flashed in her mind and took her breath away for a moment. Jessica realized that between the two of them, Boaz was a man; not a boy as Joshua still seemed to be. Boaz was also far more pleasing to her eye than Joshua. Beautiful, if you could call a man that.*

Her voice firm, she asked, "How did you find me?"

"Money is a powerful motivator," he responded.

"You mean greed is," she snapped.

"Same difference. Come, now Jessica, is that any way to greet an old friend?"

"I would rather kiss a camel!"

Jessica spun around and ran toward the door, pulling the keys from her pocket. Reaching the door, she placed the right key into the lock, turned it, and started to pull the door open. When a massive hand pushed it close, turning around rapidly, her eyes landed on her father, Matthew.

Being trapped between her father and the door gave her an uneasy, sick feeling. They both stared at each other for a time, not moving or speaking. She wondered what her father thought when he looked at her.

"You are not getting away from me this time, daughter of mine."

Before she could move or even speak, he grabbed her and pulled her around quickly with her back pressing against his chest. He took a few steps back in the process, wrapping his arm around Jessica and locking her arms at her sides. Jessica struggled to break free. Matthew's arm tightened around her as he pulled out a white cloth and held it over her nose and mouth.

Jessica tried not to breathe in the chloroform, but it was no use. She couldn't hold her breath any longer. She managed to pull from Matthew for he loosened his grip on her. She stumbled toward the door. As she reached it her legs buckled out, and she fell to the floor, passing out.

CHAPTER EIGHTEEN

A door slammed shut. The sound echoed down the hall, followed by footsteps. A few seconds later, another door opened. This one leading to a small, windowless cell where a regal, red haired woman sat on a tattered pallet. A man carrying a blanket wrapped bundle stepped inside.

"You have company," said the man. He placed his burden down on the floor gently, turned, shut and locked the door. The footsteps faded into the distance, and the echo of the door slamming again rang down the hall way. Only then did the woman crawl over to the bundle. She opened the blanket and turned a girl over. She let out a soft gasp of horror as she realized who it was.

"Oh, my dear Jessica. How did they come by you?" whispered Adele.

She lifted Jessica slightly and dragged her back to the pallet she had been on. Sitting beside her, she lifted the girl's head into her lap and leaned back against the wall. She stroked her fingers through her niece's hair; soothing them both. After a time, she fell asleep.

In the early morning hours of the following day, Jessica began to stir. Without sunlight, the only reason Adele knew that it was morning was of the tray of food someone had placed just inside the door. There was a cup of water and a bowl of fruit for each of them. Jessica let out a groan as she proceeded to sit up.

"I am glad to see you are awake."

"My head hurts," Jessica's said softly.

"That might be from the chloroform."

Adele got up, went over to the tray, brought it back over, and sat it down in between them. They ate and drank in silence for a time.

"What is going to happen?"

"They will be taking us into Libya soon."

"How do you know, and for what purpose?"

Jessica stared at her aunt, trying to gauge her reaction, but it was useless. She closed her eyes briefly, opening them again before she spoke. She ignored the first part of her niece's question, "That I do not know. But hush now, child, I need to think. Return the tray and items to the door and come back."

Jessica did as she was instructed. After a time, she couldn't keep quiet. "Will anyone come to save us?"

"I do not know the answer to that question."

She grew silent at the dismissive answer. Jessica became restless, and started to fidget a little as she began to play with her necklace. That motion got Adele's attention, and her gaze went blank for a moment before snapping back to the present.

"We will leave a trail of breadcrumbs."

"Bread crumbs, you mean like Hansel and Gretel?"

"Yes. But instead of bread crumbs, we will use our jewelry. It's about a two-month trip to get to Libya. We can use our jewelry to help with the crumbs. In that regard, I have two bracelets, a locket, and a ring," stated Adele.

"I have my anklet, a bracelet, and a necklace," Jessica replied.

"It will do just fine, but listen closely now, it has and needs to be you. Not me, but you to leave the trail, you will also have to improvise along the way. Our kidnappers will not be expecting you to do anything. They will be watching me more closely than you."

"When will I know to leave something then, if you can't help?"

"Trust me, you will know, niece. There isn't much time left. They will come for us soon."

Before she could explain further, the door opened and in stepped a younger man. Adele noted the same facial traits as Adelram, and assumed they were closely related.

"Come with me."

The women stood up and moved toward the door and out into the darkened hallway. Another man was waiting, and he led them to the steps while the other followed behind. The group stepped out into a brightly lit hall and sunlight coming through a window. It stung their eyes for a moment. Moving down this hallway to the third door and the man leading them opened it and motioned for them to enter.

"You will not be able to escape, and I would suggest you do not try," he grunted.

Jessica and Adele were shoved into the room and the door closed loudly. The sound of the door locking to echoed in the still room. Adele, stood unmoving. Jessica found her courage and, with her heart thumping loudly in her chest, stepped further into the dim room. She moved to the bed where someone had laid out some dresses. She fingered them carefully before looking up at her aunt.

Adele, by this point, met her eyes and whispered, "Go and get cleaned up, dear."

Jessica picked up the white and pink dress, she moved into the bathroom. When the door closed behind her, only then did Adele move to the bed. She knelt by the bed and began to pray fretfully. After a time, she stood up when she heard the bathroom door open and Jessica stepped out.

"Beautiful," Adele said.

Adele motioned Jessica to come over to the dressing table. There was an assortment of brushes and toiletries. Taking the boar hair brush, she began to untangle and braided the girl's hair. They said nothing the entire time. Jessica remained quiet and watched as Adele took her dress into the bathroom and shut the door behind her.

Taking advantage of this opportunity, Jessica went to the window and tried to lift it. Someone had nailed it shut. Defeated, she rested her forehead on the window and looked out.

CHAPTER NINETEEN

The door opened slowly, and a man with dark hair and eyes stood in the doorway. He was silently taking Jessica in, noticing how the sun seemed to cast a shine on her. He moved slowly over to her like a cheetah stalking its prey. Not until he was only a few feet behind her, did he speak.

"A beautiful sight, isn't it?"

Jessica spun around and froze as she saw him standing behind her. She backed slightly into the window. He took a step closer to her, with an unreadable look on his face. Jessica could only stare at him, and if she wanted to move, she wouldn't be able too. For it seemed to her that no matter how hard she tried to will herself to escape this situation, her body wouldn't respond to her silent commands.

"We should have met long before this."

"What is it that you want?" It was Adele's voice that snapped through whatever spell had a hold on her.

The man turned and looked at her aunt carefully as he responded, "We will be leaving at sundown. Get some rest."

They watched him silently as he walked out, and the door shut behind him. Jessica moved to her aunt. Adele's inhale came out as a hiss.

Images of what might have been flashed through her mind at her niece's touch. Jessica's laughter at her seventeenth birthday party. Adelram pulling her out of a burning house. Jessica kissing him while he stroked her pregnant belly. The cries of their newborn baby. Jessica's eyes held a wary gleam as her husband took control over the royal bloodline. Fire. Screams. War. Seeing her son slain, their Chieftain a prisoner. But then Adele saw Boaz comforting Jessica. A strong bond formed between them. But fear etched itself across Jessica's face as she revealed to Boaz that she was pregnant with his child.

Adele gasped at the image of Adelram's sword, splattering blood across both Jessica and Boaz's corpses. Only Jessica's daughter to Adelram survived.

Adele inhaled deeply as she stepped away from her niece. There was a slight fear in her eyes. There had been ripples in the images, and she knew there was a possibility that what she saw could come to pass. That frightened her.

Jessica stepped closer to her aunt and whispered, "Aunt Adele, what is happening to you?"

Adele turned from Jessica and took deep even breaths for some time. Jessica waited, puzzled and upset, not knowing how to handle the strange behavior from her aunt. She hardly knew her, but already she cared for her deeply. A few minutes later, Adele grabbed Jessica by the upper arms.

"Listen to me, Jessica, Boaz and the other warriors will find us. Don't give up, no matter what happens. You fight, and you keep fighting. Don't give in, please, don't give in."

"What do you mean? What is going on?"

"There is so much, and I am not at liberty to say. But know this, niece, each of us in our bloodline has a gift. A special gift."

"I don't."

"You do, and you will find it in time. Without your grandmother's guidance and teaching, along with so many other things, and it will take longer."

"I don't understand; you are speaking in riddles. And why can't you?"

Adele smiled a soft sorrowful smile and responded with regret as she spoke. "We should have met sooner."

Jessica's eyes widen as her aunt continued. "We should have met a few years ago. However, a few warriors came with me to collect you, but we arrived too late. By the time we had gotten to the port you had left. It was unfortunate timing on all our parts."

"I am sorry."

"It isn't your fault, and never you mind that now. What was done, was done. We still have hope."

Adele sighed. This time she pulled Jessica into her arms and made a silent promise that she would protect the girl from him, as long as she could fight.

"Who was that? I feel like I should know him from somewhere, but I can't remember."

Adele held a worried look and slowly answered Jessica's question. "His name is Adelram. And he is the leader of this group." She took Jessica's hands in hers and squeezed them. "What do you mean, you *know* him?"

"I don't know. It's just that he seems familiar somehow, and I can't remember why." Jessica bit her lip and added, "He made my skin crawl, and I felt heavy. Like I couldn't move. I didn't like the feeling."

She pressed a kiss to Jessica's head and whispered, "I don’t like being in his presence either child. However, he is right about one thing; we need to rest."

They moved to the bed and laid down on opposite sides. Sleep came to them eventually though it was only a couple of hours. It seemed to them they had just shut their eyes when they were harshly awakened. They were ushered out of the building, to the courtyard and then to mount the horses. The group moved out of the city. Jessica had never seen the city this late at night before, and to her it seemed like a horrible place.

As the group silently made their way out of the city gates and into the desert, they traveled north-west. Through the night and past the morning they rode. By early afternoon, they made it to one of the few oases they could come across on their journey.

The two women dismounted from their horses and stood still as their mounts were led away by two of the men. They jumped as a voice spoke directly behind them. "You may wade or swim in the water, if you like. Someone will come to collect you once the meal is ready."

He turned and walked away. They moved slowly across the camp to the water's edge. Adele sat while Jessica moved into the water about ankle deep and stood there. She was enjoying the cooling sensation against her skin. Bending down, Jessica removed her anklet so it wouldn't accidentally fall off. She held it in her fist along with handfuls of her skirt. She moved a little bit deeper into the water. Sometime later, she found Adele. No words passed between them; they were both lost in their thoughts. A gruff voice shouted out to them. Turning, they saw a chubby man standing on the bank, waving at them to come back.

Freezing just slightly Jessica spotted a rock surrounded by reeds, seeing an opportune moment, she allowed her aunt to stand in front of her so she could use her as a shield. She dropped the anklet on the surface of the rock as she moved past it.

Then she picked up her pace slightly to catch up with her aunt. They soon found themselves sitting on the ground with bowls of food. Jessica wrinkled her nose at the roasted meat, and she picked and pushed at it. She saw her aunt doing the same thing, rather than eating. She leaned over to whisper to Adele.

"Is this pork?" Jessica wrinkled her nose. "Not eating it. Very uncooth it is."

Turning at her niece's words, Adele smiled as she followed suit.

They sat their bowls down. A cold shiver went down their spines as a voice spoke up from behind them. "Food not to your liking?" asked Adelram.

Jessica opened her mouth to speak. Adele gave her a warning look, and Jessica bit her lower lip and remained silent.

As her aunt stood and faced Adelram.

"Is there anything else that is more to your liking, perhaps?" He asked with a sinister smile.

"No. Nothing," was Adele's response to the man before her.

"Come, I will show you to your resting place."

They followed Adelram to a small shaded area with bedrolls laid out for them. After they stepped inside, they heard him command some men to stand guard. Time passed, and sunset found the camp breaking up and preparing to depart. Before long, the two women were back on the horses, their hands tied to the horn of the saddle as the group rode into the night.

They moved slowly through the desert. That night the wind seemed to be blowing a little harder than previous nights, causing near-blind conditions. They had no choice but to make camp under the shelter of a plateau ledge, staying as close to it as they could. They used the tents to block out the blowing sand. Adele curled herself around Jessica, offering her niece as much protection as possible.

The group drifted in and out of sleep due to the howling of the wind. Jessica managed to remove one of Adele's bracelets and pushed it up against the wall of the plateau. It was the middle of the next day when the wind calmed. They found themselves back on the horses and moving again, starting at a full pace to make up for the lost time. At dusk the next day, the group dismounted and ate the ripe dates they had. Bedrolls were laid out, and the women fell asleep while someone stood watch.

When they woke the next day, they did not stop until mid-afternoon at another oasis. This time the women were allowed to wash and bathe. They even cleaned their clothes and hid among the reeds until their clothes dried. Jessica found a sharp rock and managed to tear a small piece of fabric from her dress. She walked along the the water's edge. Glancing around quickly to make sure no one was watching, she placed the fabric and a rock on top of it.

The next twenty-two days passed in the same way: Jessica trying to leave clues whenever they stopped. More often than not, she couldn't, and worry gnawed at her insides. They managed on the twenty-third day that the group reached the Nile River. While the supplies and horses were being loaded on to some rafts.

Jessica walked a short distance away and sat on the sandy banks of the Nile, with her shoes off and her feet in the cold water. Jessica took some stones with the help of the sand left a beautiful design of Celtic knot, along with a couple of pictures, one was a flower and the other a leaf. She pulled her knees up to her chest and stared out over the water with silent tears trailing down her face.

How long she sat there, she didn't know, but soon she felt a shadow fall over her, and a voice spoke. "I see you have a talent."

She scrambled to her feet, took a step away from him, and almost fell back. But the man grabbed her before she could hurt herself, and pulled her up onto the bank. He gestured for her to get her shoes, and she walked back beside him. They came back to the group. She was given a small ration and water to drink before she was ushered on to the raft. They began to move across the river.

CHAPTER TWENTY

The river crossing was a peaceful one, and Jessica was soon lulled to sleep by the gentle rocking of the raft. At some point the next day, she woke up from a deep sleep. Riding in front of her aunt, she realized she'd been carried off the raft. This made her feel vulnerable, helpless, and she sank into her aunt even more. She closed her eyes again as a headache began to assault her, and buried her face into her aunt's arms to avoid the light.

Her aunt whispered in her ear. "I know dearest. The heat is getting to you."

All she could to in response, was nod and close her eyes.

~~~

Adele looked at her niece in concern. She frowned, her eyes narrowed in thought, and braced herself for a battle as she went looking for Adelram. She didn't want her niece anywhere near him. She also knew that as sick as her niece was getting, he was her only option. She knew they would be passing by Mallawi. But they had to stop, and there was no other way.

She turned on her heel and marched quickly across the camp until she found the brothers under the shade of a few trees. She noted her nephew was them and she let out a growl of anger. She took a few deep breathes and schooled her face into a passive one. before moving over to them. Her voice was sharp, "Adelram, a word in private."

"Of course, Lady Adele."
~~~

They moved away from the group and back across towards Jessica. "What do you see?" was her words to him.

Adelram looked at the sleeping young woman. He took in her flushed face and fevered look. He slowly turned to Adele before he spoke. "We need to make a stop in Mallawi to get her help." With these words, she turned and looked at him with a hardened expression, as she continued, "Unless, you want the princess to die."

His eyes narrowed at her, and she didn't break his gaze. It seemed like neither would back down. "Sir?"

A nervous voice sounded from behind them, and they both turned and said, "What?"

The two glanced at each other before Adele moved away and sat down beside Jessica. Before long they were back on their horses, Jessica was enclosed in her aunt's arms again, and they moved onward. It was another two days before they found themselves in the city of Mallawi.

They found the nearest hotel and checked in. At the front desk, Adelram asked for a doctor to be brought for the young woman. There was nothing the doctor could do. She needed to be kept cold with plenty of water and rest. For if she was left out in the sun any longer, she wouldn't have survived it. The doctor abruptly left.

It was a week before Jessica was showing improvement. On the eighth day, she took a candle from the room and broke it in half, and wrote a short message on it. She tied the paper to the candle, and hid it in her skirt pocket, then she proceeded to light the bottom of the candle. An hour later, with just a stub left, Jessica was blowing it out as there was a knock at the door.

"Jessica." She heard her aunt's voice, moved quickly toward the door, and opened it. "Take the back steps down when you get outside, take the side alley way to the gate. Place your item in sight from the road on the right side of the gate under the bush, and hurry back. There isn't much time."

Jessica frowned at Adele. She wanted to question her about how she knew every step Jessica should take. However, Adele shooed her away quickly. So, Jessica found herself running and stumbling a little to get to the gate. She placed the candle right where her aunt said before she hurried back to the hotel room. Adele quickly opened the door and pulled Jessica in by her arm. She ushered her niece into the bathroom and promptly undressed her. Adele pushed Jessica into the tub and told her to bathe herself.

Jessica stared at the door quizzically for a time before stepping into the water to do as asked. Halfway through, she heard the sound of male voices competing with her aunt's. Jessica finished bathing and got out. She found a folded, clean dress on the dressing table with undergarments. The dress was relatively simple. The top of it was a turquoise color with a corset. The turquoise color flowed into ivory lace for the bottom skirt. The sleeves were short and puffed.

When she opened the door, she heard her aunt's voice. "She needs shoes, hers were left behind."

"She will have to deal with it. We've wasted too much time as it is."

"Don't you dare-!"

Jessica cleared her voice to stop the argument. She felt the danger to her aunt, and it angered her. At her slight noise, all eyes turned to her and she shifted uncomfortably. Adelram slowly raked his gaze up and down her form before saying anything. He was irritated, but something else glittered in his eyes.

"We are leaving. Now!"

He turned to the door and stormed out. Jessica found a hair ribbon and pulled her hair back into a bun quickly. She followed her aunt as they moved towards the hot, stone street. Before she could reach it, another man picked her up swiftly and lifted her to her horse. Without another word, they started to move out of the city.

By sunset the next day, they found themselves drinking water from canteens and eating more dates. The men brushed down, watered, and fed the horses and camels. Before they set out again, Jessica left her aunt's second bracelet at an oasis on a rock amid some reeds. All too soon, they found themselves on another plateau, moving along carefully. Adele whispered, "We are over halfway to Libya by now. Soon we will cross over; under two days if I am not mistaken. I pray that help will soon come."

Jessica looked at her aunt, puzzled. She answered her niece's unspoken question. "There are some undercurrents, tensions between the two countries that could erupt at any time. It's very dangerous crossing the border these days; many have perished."

"Perish?"

"Lawlessness in the area means that bandits and armed, violent men are much more brazen than ever. There are many clashes between tribal authorities who reside in the area with military personnel. And often."

Jessica considered everything and stared straight ahead, in silence. Later that morning, they paused to rest after the long, difficult trek down the cliff. At that time, Jessica took off her bracelet and slipped it under her pillow. She lay awake, praying. A few hours later, Adelram and two others met nearby where they spoke in hushed tones.

"We are making good time, despite the sand storm and the girl being sick," a man said.

"Yes, we have been fortunate in that regard, Tony," Adelram agreed.

"What is the next phase, brother?" asked the second one.

"We have two more full days to travel. Once we enter into Libya there is a small village where we'll stop to rest. From there we head to Aj Jaghbub; it's the first city we will come across. The rest you both know. Get some sleep. We'll need to be alert; we'll need all of our skills when we cross the border."

The two men nodded, not daring to argue with their older brother and leader. They walked directly past Jessica and her sleeping aunt. Jessica froze. She couldn't move from the spot after what she heard, and she curled herself into a ball. With her eyes tightly closed, she forced herself to take slow, deep breathes as she still felt eyes on her. She wanted whoever was watching her to believe she was asleep. Eventually, she heard them move away and the feeling of being watched slowly eased.

Dawn broke the following day, and they found themselves traveling again. They arrived at another oasis in the early evening. It was bigger than the last two they'd stopped at. The group of men bustled to set up tents and build two small campfires, while sentries were chosen to guard the camp. The two women dismounted and stood where they were told. They never argued or strayed; they were too wise to risk it.

The fear and tension inside the camp was thick, and the voices of the men hushed and quiet around them. Finally, someone approached them. "Your tent has been set up and some food has been made ready." He abruptly motioned for them to come with him.

They followed him across the camp to a tent and were happy to disappear inside. In the middle of the floor was a low, rough makeshift table, with two bowls and cups. Two cots were set up off to the side with a pillow and blanket on each. On top of the blankets, there were fresh clothes. A few feet away from the cots was a wash basin, two large jars filled with water, towels and washcloths, a bottle of oil and a cake of soap.

Jessica worked up her courage and moved to the cots to study the dresses.

> They were both a teal color, with a satin-trimmed neckline and puffed half-sleeves with draw strings. Embroidered and princess seamed, they had a cross-laced at the bodice, with a smocked back panel and ties at the waist for a flattering fit.

"They remind me a little bit of home." Spoke Jessica softly as she held one up for her aunt to look at, her aunt nodded her head in agreement.

"Let's freshen up and see what they left us to eat."

It took time to bathe; each having to help the other. Once they dried off and dressed, Adele brushed and braided Jessica's long hair. In turn, Jessica fixed her aunt's hair and they both felt much better. They slowly moved over to the low table, where they found a pitcher of water, fruits, bread, and a broth. Adele sat and paused as she looked at food thoughtfully. By now, Jessica had poured the water into the cups and tried to hand one to Adele. She noticed the far-off look.

Reaching over, she shook her aunt lightly to get her attention. Adele blinked and smiled at Jessica as she took the cup. "Thank you, dear."

Jessica poured broth into the bowls and shared the fruit. Adele tore a few pieces of bread and motioned Jessica to take her hand as she spoke. "Great God, Thou Giver of all good, accept our praise and bless our food. Grace, health, and strength to us afford Through Jesus Christ, our blessed Lord. Amen."

As Adele started to speak, Jessica bowed her head. In a few seconds, Adele finished praying.

"Amen," whispered Jessica.

They started to eat, pausing as she reached the cup of water. She saw her aunt sitting there still, just tapping the spoon against the table absent mindedly.

"Are you not eating?"

"Sorry, child, I was lost in thought."

Adele slowly began to eat. Finally, Jessica had a drink of water. A few minutes later, she whispered, "I am not feeling too good."

She tried to stand but fell as her legs gave out. Quickly acting, Adele stood up and grabbed her before she could injure herself and gently laid her down. She sat back at her place and whispered out loud, "What are you playing at Adelram?" She exhaled slowly as she picked up her glass and drank some of the tainted drink. As it took hold, she laid down, reached out, and clasped Jessica's hand. Everything went black.

CHAPTER TWENTY-ONE

The first rays of sunset found Jessica stirring and rolling over. As she sat up slowly, she turned and tried to shake her aunt awake. She realized her aunt was still in a very deep sleep. She stood up as she surveyed the tent; the towels and items they had used to bathe were gone, as well as the dishes. There was a fresh water jug and cup on the table. Suddenly, she noticed a pressing need, so, tearing a little bit of her dress, she moved to the corner. After relieving herself, she went back to the table and poured water over her hands.

Jessica wished she had some soap, but water would do for now. A strange, low, hissing began near the corner where she relieved herself. Jessica slowly turned to see what was making the sound, and moved the rug. There among a sand-covered rock, were some ugly and evil-looking snakes that were hissing very angrily.

Inspiration overcame Jessica, and she quickly went back to her aunt and removed the locket. She then found a small, sharp, stone. She flipped the pendant over and started to leave a message; or tried to. All she could fit was Aj Jag. It was hard to make out, but it would have to do, she thought, and she moved back to the snakes.

~~~

Adele woke up in the meantime, and wondering the commotion was. *What was*
~~~

that girl fussing over? Suddenly, her eyes widened as she saw the snakes. She knew that breed of snake; the Egyptian Cobra. Not just one but a nest of them, and they were deadly.

Adele scrambled to her feet with no time to lose. Before she could reach her, Jessica had thrown the locket into the nest. She stumbled back as one of the snakes struck at her. But the deed was done; it bit Jessica on her thigh.

Adele screamed, frantically.

Quickly Adele began to throw whatever she could at the snakes. She threw the pitcher at them, and although it didn't kill anything, the distraction worked. The snakes turned their attention to Adele.

CHAPTER TWENTY-TWO

A man rushed into the tent and saw the angry snake getting ready to strike Adele. Risking a clear shot, he raised his gun, and a shot rang out. The cobra dropped dead on the ground. He watched as Adele rushed to Jessica's side. She moved the skirt of her dress out of the way, and he spotted the bite. Then he took notice of the venom already starting to take hold.

He holstered his pistol and grabbed Jessica by the wrists, pulling her out of the tent. Adelle ran out behind him. They laid Jessica on the ground as several hired men appeared, alarmed by the noise. He sprinted towards the supply tent, shouting to one of them to find his two brothers. Breathless, he made the last several yards toward the medical supplies. Grabbing the anti-venom kit, he dashed back across the camp. He didn't spare any time as he dropped to his knees beside her. He quickly opened the bag, prepared the antidote, and injected it right above the bite. He then moved her further away from the tent. Adele followed and sat on the ground beside her, holding her hand.

In his peripheral vision, he could see his brothers approaching, their brows furrowed with concern. The man lifted his hand from Jessica's forehead, ignoring his brothers for the moment. He removed a handkerchief from around his neck and poured water from his canteen onto it. He set the cool, wet material on her forehead. Turning back, he met his older brothers' gazes carefully. The older clearly had a million questions, while his oldest brother glared at him with fierce impatience.

"What *happened,* Caleb?" asked Adelram.

"We were lucky with the quick thinking of Lady Adele," Caleb said and nodded his head in Adele's direction. "The heiress got bitten by a venomous snake. What kind I don't know." He pointed over his shoulder. "The nest is in the tent."

"It's an Egyptian cobra," Adele said, her eyes never leaving Jessica's face.

The brothers shared a look before sending one of the men inside to find the snakes. The unfortunate fellow could hardly see, but quickly stepped on the dead reptile. He got out of the tent as fast as he could, tossing the carcass on the ground at Adelram's feet.

"Find the ones responsible and bring them to me, Tony," Adelram said.

Tony bowed, turned, and went about finding them. A few short minutes passed, that seemed to be a lifetime. When he returned, he had a pole in hand and two nervous men with him. He took the pole into the tent while Adelram questioned the two men as to why they failed in their duties.

Tony found the nest and gently lifted one of the snakes. He moved slowly back toward the group, stopping a few paces away. He looked at Caleb and nodded his head toward the two men. Caleb stepped back as he figured out what Tony had in mind. He backed slowly away as the conversation between Adelram and the two men finished. They apologized emphatically.

"Not good enough," said Tony. Everyone's attention turned to him. He threw the snake at the two men when they turned around.

The man let out a terrified scream as the snake landed on him and bit down on his shoulder and neck area. He stumbled backward and fell to the ground; the snake slithered away quickly. The three brothers looked on with cold indifference as the man began to scream and convulse. Within a few short minutes he was dead.

Adele had a sad and horrific look on her face with a hand over her mouth.

The other hired man was trembling in fear. As Adelram turned his cold gaze upon him and smiled. "Run!"

The man stuttered, "Yes Sir!" and made a hasty retreat.

Adelram removed his handgun and shot him. He fell face down in the sand, dead. Adelram shrugged and casually stepped over him. The rest of the men stood frozen as they saw two of their own dead. A moment later Tony and Caleb threw the other body out top of him.

"Get rid of these bodies! And break camp!" Adelram ordered as he stalked away.

Soon after the camp was broken down, they rode away. A snake in the nest slithered away, and the locket glimmer in the sunlight.

~~~

Evening fell, and by mid-morning of the next day, Jessica awakened in the arms of her aunt on a horse. "You foolish, foolish girl, what were you thinking, going near that nest for, have you lost your senses?"
~~~

"I'm sorry," Jessica said. Adele hugged the girl tighter to her.

After an hour, the girl whispered. "Can we walk?"

Tony heard the girl's quiet question and moved quickly from beside her. Jessica watched him move to the front of the line and closed her eyes. Five minutes later, she opened them again, at the feel of a grip on her wrist.

She opened her eyes and saw a man riding beside them. Jessica began pulling her arm back toward her. The man's voice was sharp, "Don't pull."

Finally, he let her wrist go and place his wrist across her forehead and nodded to himself. "Your fever is breaking, and your pulse is stronger. You may walk for a time. If you both need to rest, tug your rope, and the ones holding it will put you back on the horse."

Jessica spoke before aunt could, and with gratefulness in her voice. "Thank you."

He didn't say anything but waited for them to dismount, and the rope that bounded her aunt's hands was tied to another rope as well as Jessica's hands. He gave the men in charge of the lines a strict warning about making sure they get water and if they needed to stop, to have them get back on the horse.

Caleb urged his horseback to the front of the group, missing the two men rolling their eyes at his back as they moved their horses forward again. Jessica watched the two men nervously, considering their actions. But they started to walk, and Jessica focused on her surroundings. It was a great feeling to be walking again.

Jessica's relief was short-lived, however, when she started to notice the faster pace. It wasn't until they became thirsty and began to stumble that they both realized that the two men were ignoring the orders given to them. Jessica tripped and braced herself for impact, but Adele helped her stay upright.

"Aunt Adele, what do we do?"

"Try to keep moving," she responded as her grave gaze locked with Jessica for a moment before she stumbled. She maintained her balance, and they both focused on trying to keep up with the pace.

Jessica kept stumbling over the uneven ground and eventually loosing balance and found herself being dragged through sand and dirt. Jessica squeezed her eyes shut as the dirt and stones scraped her clothes and skin. She barely heard her aunt cry out for them to hold a moment. But the two men didn't slow down or even look behind.

Jessica felt her aunt trying to help her, but both women ended up being dragged across the ground. The rough surface was more than she could bear. Tears blurred Jessica's vision, and she screamed as loud as she could.

Suddenly a voice, furious, boomed over the sound of the horses.

"I gave you an order. What is the meaning of this?" Caleb growled as he and Tony sliced through their ropes, bringing everything to a halt.

Jessica pushed herself up despite the pain and crawled over to her aunt.

Tony swung down from his horse. Took his knife and cut through the bonds, glaring at the two men.

Jessica pulled Adele into her lap. "Are you alright?" With trembling, bleeding fingers, Jessica removed Adele's ring, her tears falling on the small cuts on her aunt's face.

"Thank you, dear." Adele offered a pained smile as Jessica tried wiping the blood off her face with the edge of her dress. Jessica didn't get a chance to reply. Caleb held out his canteen. "You need to drink."

With hands still shaking, Jessica took the canteen and had her aunt drink from it. Then she did the same. Caleb took the container back and poured the other half in equal amounts onto their hands and foreheads to help cool them. He took in Jessica's pale face with a worried look. Turning his head slightly, he noticed Adelram and her father rode up to them, though the latter stayed back, stone-faced.

"Will you both be alright for a moment?" Caleb whispered.

All Jessica could do was nod her head in confusion at him. Caleb scowled as he pulled Adelram aside. Jessica strained to hear their words but could only catch Caleb's harsh tone. Judging by Adelram's shrug and smug expression, she guessed the situation didn't upset him as it did Caleb. She saw Adelram shake his head like a parent would scold a child.

"No one deserves that!" Caleb shouted. He spun around and fired two shots at the disobedient men. Both fell from their horses with a bullet through their chests.

Jessica gasped. Caleb turned to her. "I didn't realize they were family to the men we killed back at the camp, or I wouldn't have assigned them."

"I will deal with you later." Adelram glowered at Caleb. "We've wasted enough time. Let's move. Tony, take the Lady Adele. I will take heiress for the last leg of our journey."

Jessica clenched her aunt's ring tightly in her lap as she sat rigidly in front of Adelram. She focused on watching Tony's horse ahead of them to avoid thinking about how the man's body pressed into hers. It wasn't long before they made it to the border and started down the rocky plateau.

She discreetly let Adele's ring drop to the ground. Her aunt's warning troubled her already frightening thoughts, but Jessica couldn't fight the urge forever and slumped against her captor in an uneasy sleep.

CHAPTER TWENTY-THREE

By late evening, they came upon the outskirt of the village. Adele had been awake for a short time and took in the village leaders that stood and waited for them as they approached. Adelram halted the party and gave a traditional greeting. The leaders did likewise as one moved forward.

"Welcome. Lodges have been made ready for your group, and you and your family will be staying at my home."

Adelram nodded his head. "I thank thee for your hospitality. My household and I are honored to stay in this beautiful village."

As soon as Tony helped Adele dismount, she rushed over to Adelram's horse with a guarded expression. "Jessica, wake up, my dear." She held out her hands for her niece. Jessica rubbed the sleep from her eyes. She took Adele's hands and slid into her aunt's warm embrace.

Adelram dismounted and led the way with the women behind him, followed by his brothers and Jessica's Father. They soon came to a large tent. Stepping inside, they saw it was a straightforward dwelling.

The few items of luxury that could be noted screamed money to Jessica. She wondered if this was the leader of the village homes. Her eyes landed on a young man and a girl that looked to be about her age.

The man sat at a chair near a small table and a girl sitting on the floor beside him. In his one hand holding a book and the other hand rested on her head. But their eyes now rested upon them. The man who led them inside gave a sharp order at the girl. Had her stand up and she motioned Jessica and her aunt to follow.

The girl showed Adele to her chamber for the night. Then Jessica followed the girl to her room, she went to a chest and pulled out two-night dresses, handed one to Jessica, and motioned her over to a small bathing tub than left after what seemed like a lifetime of waiting.

The girl finally came in with two buckets of warm water and proceeded to dump the water into the tub, then left. Jessica turned and looked at the cover entrance and stripped. Kneeling beside the tub, Jessica ducked her head and proceeded to wash and rinse. Then she stepped in and bath by the time she was done, dried, and dress in the cream nightgown.

The girl came back in, smiled, and proceeded to take the tub out with help from an older woman. Then she returned with the empty container. She handed Jessica a brushed. Jessica brushed and braided her hair off to the side.

Jessica stared at the girl for a time and wondered if she knew how to speak English, taking a deep breath to find out she spoke, "What is your name? Mine is Jessica," her voice held an unsure tone in it.

"Mine is Lina." The words were halting as if the girl had to think about each word first.

"How do you know the English tongue? We had to learn in our school."

"I learned from my future husband," respond Lina, and the girls looked at each other for a time in uneasiness before lying down to sleep.

Just before dawn, Lina awakened to the sound of soft crying. Rolling over, she saw that it was Jessica struggling in the middle of a dream. She moved over and shook her awake. Jessica flew up quickly, and they bumped heads, groaned, and rubbed their forehead. Jessica whispered, "Sorry. What is wrong?"

"You had a bad dream. Do you want to talk about it?"

Jessica pulled her knees up and stared ahead, a few minutes later responded with, "I am scared not only for myself but for my aunt. I suppose I was dreaming about it."

"Fears?"

"My aunt and I were taking from our families. I pray that my aunt's people will find us and soon. Do you have any paper and a fountain pen?"

"Will return in a moment." Lina left the room quickly and moved silently into another bedroom.

~~~

Lina moved to the desk, she reached for the pen first, then froze when the room's occupant spoke quietly, "Lina."

Slowly, she went to bed, as the male set up as she sat down beside him. "Faris."

"Lina."

She smiled as she laid against him, her head on his chest.

"What are you doing. If you get caught, I can't keep you safe. I will not have you pay the price for what your mother has done and the shame she brought onto this family."

"I am nothing like her."
~~~

"I know, but he will not see it that way."

"I understand. I am getting writing items for Jessica, the girl that is rooming with me. I want to help her, Faris. She and her aunt were taken from their family, and the girl is certain that they are coming for them."

"That is a heavy charge she is claiming. Be extremely careful if that is the truth. Hurry back to your room before you are discovered inside my room."

Lina nodded her head against his chest. Before placing a light kiss on his jawbone before getting up and grabbing the items she came in for and left. Going back into her room, she lit the oil lamp and trimmed to where it is low. By now, the sun had started to peak on the horizon.

Lina handed Jessica the paper and pen.

~~~

Jessica snatched both from her hands and started to write.

Boaz or whom it concerns,

If Adele has any close kin inside her husband's family, then I give the title that grandmamma gave me as the Favor One. Whatever that means. If anything does happen to us. The pendant is proof of that. We will be leaving into that city today; I am sure of it. I hope this finds you soon enough.

Sincerely,

Jessica Piper McKinney

Pausing, as a few teardrops hit the paper. Jessica wiped them away quickly. She gripped her necklace tightly for a short time. Slowly proceeded to unclasp the chain and placed it in the center of the letter, carefully folded up the paper so that all edges were tucked under and the necklace wouldn't slip out. Taking a deep breath, she turned to the girl. Uneasily Lina shifted as she realized Jessica was going to ask her something.
~~~

"Would you be willing to give it to the ones who are searching for us?"

"How do you know they will come?"

"Faith and hope that is in my heart."

"If they pass through this way. The only problem is, I don't know who I am looking for."

Jessica looked at her for a moment, finding the right words to use. "They will be men." *Great Jessica*, she thought to herself, *state the obvious.* She moved on quickly. "They will be dressed in dark clothes. A few of them will have a symbol that they are wearing."

Lina held up her hand in warning as male voices was heard close to the curtain of the room and going past. Lina quickly stood and expressed, "I will bring you a light breakfast and some fresh clothes to wear."

Jessica watched Lina leave the room, and she stood slowly. She wondered if she should find Adele or stay put. Jessica edged slowly to the door and peered around the curtain to the central part of the home.

There sat many men; one of them that stood out was her proud Father eating with them as the small conversation was held in inaudible words that drifted to her ears.

Letting the curtain fall back into place. Jessica moved to the place where she slept and sat down. Pulling the blanket up and around her shoulders, she sat there for how long she didn't know. Eventually, Lina came back with a change of clothes for her like she promised and left immediately.

Standing, Jessica shed her clothes and picked up the ones she'd been given. Shaking out the clothes, she realized it was a long wrap dress that made from brown linen and closed with two ribbons. Lina came back in and saw that the girl was having issues putting the dress on.

Lina placed the light breakfast on her small table. Turning, Lina moved over to Jessica and helped her into the dress, and closed it with the two ribbons. Lina moved to the other side of the room and opened up a drawer in the small table where the oil lamp was. Digging through the drawer, Lina finally pulled out a lighter color brown cloth.

Jessica realized it was a sash that had decorative stitching on it, and she placed that around Jessica's waist and tied it in the back.

"Come, I made you some breakfast. Have you ever had ta'ameya be before?"

Jessica shook her head, no in response.

"Then you are in for a treat. It's made with dried fava beans. We make ours with parsley, cilantro, poblano, and yellow onion, to name a few of the ingredients."

It was served inside a piece of grainy pita bread. Jessica wondered if it was like the Pita bread back in Midbar Shemesh. *It might not be so bad, and it does look good.* Jessica thought to herself as she took hold of it and bit into it.

Jessica ate slowly but couldn't finish and looking into Lina's eyes and voice her thoughts on the taste. "I can't bear to finish the rest of this breakfast. It was good, but I don't think I care for the full spiciness of it. Thank you for taking the time to make it for me."

Lina smiled and responded, "Most welcome. Come, it's nearly time for you to leave."

Lina and Jessica stared at each other for the most extended moment. Lina drew Jessica into a hug and whispered in her ear, "I will keep my eye out every hour, and every day, I will try not to fail you or your aunt. My friend."

"Thank you."

"Jessica? You ready dear, it's time to go." Adele's voice sounded outside the curtain.

"Coming."

"Good." Adele walked away.

Jessica took a few breaths to settle nerves and headed outside. She was stepping into the morning light and blinked and shielded her eyes with her hand. Taking in the village that she didn't see the evening before last.

"Move, daughter." The cold, deep voice of her father sounded behind her.

Jessica took in a deep breath. "Why are you doing this? What was said to you to make you give me up? Did you and mother ever love me? Or is my mother ashamed of who her family is, and I remind her of them? Or are you not even my father?"

"You speak of matters that don't concern you, and you have no idea what you're saying." He brushed past her.

"Even before I was born?" She called after him.

Matthew turned the few yards he had traveled and looked at her, "Happy we were. Did we love you? No."

Tears slowly fell from her eyes as she stared after him and her heartbreak, *after all this time she still had hope, but to hear it said was more than she could bear.* She watched him walk away. Matthew stopped a few more paces away, turning he marched back, grabbed her arm forcefully, and dragged her behind him. Then and only then did she barely get the words out.

"My pendant, the one grandmamma gave me is gone, I need to find it! The latch must have become loose. Let me go, please."

She tugged fruitlessly on her arm, but he didn't break his hold, and when Matthew made it to Adele, he flung his youngest at the woman. Adele caught her sobbing niece, and her eyes narrowed at the man who was supposed to be her nephew. They felt no bond between them. Her voice held no emotion, only steel.

"Nephew."

He regarded her with a sneer before spinning away and walking toward his horse. Adele's gaze left the retreating form and looked softly down upon the young lady in her arms and spoke, "What happened, my dearest?"

All Jessica could do was shake her head. A few minutes later, the brothers moved forward, Caleb placed Jessica sideways on his horse as he mounted the horse behind her. Adele rode with Tony, and they advanced onward to the city of Aj Jaghbub. The last days of the journey were quiet with stops of rest until the mid-afternoon on the last day. They made it into the city, and moved to one of the hotels.

Adelram went in, and a few minutes later, came out and waved to the group to dismount. The group entered the hotel and was led upstairs, the hired men stayed on the first floor.

The worker proceeded up another flight of stairs to the next landing and a few keys to Adelram and left. Standing before them were ten women ranging in age. Jessica's heart started to pound, and fear began to gnaw at her insides as she trembled. Her aunt remained stoic as ever.

Five of the women moved to them. The youngest woman in the group grabbed Jessica firmly on her arm and pulled her away from her aunt. Jessica began to struggle. The men looked on with amusement in their eyes. Jessica didn't pay them any attention as she tried to reach for her aunt again, crying.

Slowly the five women managed to get the girl away and pulled her down the hall and into a room. At the same time, the other women escorted Adele into her room.

When the door closed behind Jessica, she stood like a statue. A bath was prepared, oils and items laid out. Before she could move or do anything, a woman came over and helped her undress. All the while she stood petrified. Jessica soon found herself in a warm bath with oils, and she soaked for hours or so it seemed.

Two of the women came back in and helped her out. With not so gentle hands, they took her to another smaller tub and poured jars of warm water over her. They washed and scrubbed her down, even shaved her. When they finished, she was wrapped in a warm blanket and forced on her stomach on the bed as they began to massage oils into her body both front and back.

This treatment had Jessica blushing with embarrassment and horror. By nightfall, they had her hair brushed and hung loosely, and dressed her and a white nightgown. They led her from the room and down the hall a little further. Opening the door and pushing her in before closing it quickly behind her.

Jessica saw her aunt by the fireplace, and their eyes connected. The next second, Jessica rushed into her aunt's arms and tucked her head into her aunt. They stood still, never realizing that the glow from the fireplace revealed the outline of their bodies through the light gowns they wore.

Matthew stood from the table, nodded his head to Adelram, "I will take my leave now.

"Of course, Lord McKinney."

Matthew nodded his head and left the room quickly, only pausing just slightly near his daughter. It was so small a gesture that Jessica thought she imagined it, as he continued to the door and shut it behind him.

The quiet conversation seemed to drift between the three brothers, and every so often, their eyes strayed to the two women. All three took in the women's features and body shapes for a time. Soon the conversation died away, and both Caleb and Tony stood.

"We will take our leave as well, brother. Enjoy your time tonight," said Tony.

CHAPTER TWENTY-FOUR

Adelram just smirked at them. They left the room. Adelram just sat at the table, sipping his wine slowly. Adele had grown tense as she tried to plan what to do. Seeing the tray on the table, she mentally prepared herself as she saw Adelram stand.

Adelram stood and drained the rest of his wine, and again, he sauntered towards the two women. His eyes slowly moved from the young girl and rested on Adele's. He very well knew that the older one would be the handful, and needed to be taken care of first. He circled them like a hunter, trailing his hands on them slowly.

The young girl shivered, and he smiled darkly at her response. As he was expecting Adele sprung to action as she pushed the heiress away roughly and twirling around, she glanced at Adelram in a challenge. They silently sized the other up for a second time, trying to gauge the other's reaction.

They circled each other slowly over and over again. Adele was finally in reach of the table with her back to it so that she could grab the tray. Adele watched as Jessica moved to a corner and huddled.

Adele spun and grabbed the tray, the wine bottle shattered as it hit the edge of the table and floor. Ignoring all that, she met Adelram's attack head-on. Adele ground her teeth together, for the vibration from the hit of the sword. She knew there wouldn't be much of a fight, but she had to stall just long enough to buy a little bit of time. There were blocks and hits by both parties. Jessica gasped in horror as her aunt lost the tray.

Adele motioned for Jessica to stay put and, in the next second, grabbed Adelram's wrist, and kneed him in the thigh, which made him stumble back. She quickly grabbed the tray, realizing just how close they were to Jessica.

Adele dodged left and turned back closer to the fireplace. Adelram came down on her and managed to knock the tray out of her hands. She moved backward and backed herself into a corner. He whispered to her, "You and the girl belong to me."

Adele spit at him, and he backed handed her roughly. As her head hit the edge of the cinder bricks on the fireplace, everything blacked out. Her eyes closed and a last thought drifted through Adele's mind, *'Please help God.'*

~~~

Jessica stood frozen as she watched her aunt crumple to the ground, caught by Adelram. He moved her to the middle of the floor. She observed as the man bent over Adele and tore her gown away from her and
~~~

spread her legs. Was overcome with fear, her eyes widened in horror. She let out a broken whisper.

"No!"

Seeing her aunt and her past self-merge ever so slightly, she couldn't let this happen to someone else. Quickly glancing around, she noticed a side table with a vase of flowers on it. Jessica was moving swiftly and softly to the jar. Hesitating only slightly, reaching for the vase of flowers. She grabbed it and turned toward Adelram. Coming up behind him, he saw her shadow and turned before he could react. She slammed the vase down on his head with tears in her eyes.

"No, no playing house. No more, please."

Jessica pushed Adelram off of her aunt and slowly dragged her aunt across the room to the farthest wall with a window. Jessica started to shake her aunt, trying to wake her up but couldn't. She was afraid she had died. Jessica placed her ear on her chest, felt her heartbeat, and slow breathing. She begged her aunt to wake up.

Jessica fought back tears. Looking around the room, she noticed the door. Biting her lip, she moved quickly to the opposite side of the room. Opening the door, a crack, she peeked through and saw a few armed men standing there.

Jessica quickly shut the door. Turning around, she ran to the window, looked out and noticed how far they were up but saw ledges. Thinking immediately, she tried to open the window. Slowly but surely struggling, she managed to move it a couple of inches. Pausing a few seconds, she started her task again.

CHAPTER TWENTY-FIVE

Adelram grunted and pushed himself up. Looking around, he saw the window open halfway, and the girl still struggling with it. He watched amused, as she turned slightly to look behind her and find him standing there with a dark look on his face. He grabbed her and tossed her onto the bed. "You want to play rough, little princess? Then rough you will get."

Adelram laughed as Jessica pulled herself up and started to scramble to the other side of the bed. Effortlessly, he reached down and latched on to her ankle to pull her back to him.

Adelram was upon her in a blink of an eye, pressing into her. His right hand yanked on her hair and pulled her head back. He saw the terror in her eyes and slammed his lips onto hers.

Struggling, Jessica let out a muffled cry. Adelram felt a sharp sting before the taste of blood on his tongue interrupted him. He forced Jessica onto her back and grabbing the girl's wrists, pinned them above her head. He leaned forward and sucked on her ear lobe for a moment, before whispering in her ear, "You and your aunt belong to me now, Princess. With time you will yearn not only for my touch, but that of my brothers."

"Never," she hissed.

"Oh, you will see, Your Highness. You will."

Adelram started to trail kisses down her neck to her chest and sucked on her breast, as Jessica began to cry and struggle. He moved back up upon her neck and sucked there before pulling away and standing.

Adelram watched as the princess rolled herself off the mattress and into the corner where she curled up, sobbing. Undressing, he moved to stand over her. Jessica looked up fearfully and cringed, trying to press herself further into the wall.

Adelram pulled her to her feet and laughed as she tried to hit him. He liked the fight she put up. With a smirk, he shoved her roughly against the wall holding her there with his bodyweight, and tore her gown in two. Then, he tossed her back onto the bed like a rag doll. Tired of waiting, he was on top of her again.

Jessica's mind flooded with horrible memories. Through her sobs she pleaded, "I don't want to play house."

Adelram ignored Jessica's crying and pleading, roughly tying her hands to the bedpost with his sash. He leaned back and watched in sick amusement as she struggled.

~~~

Jessica closed her eyes as she realized the sash was too tight. Fear tremored through her and she whimpered in spite of herself. As she locked her legs together as tightly as she could, he pressed his body into hers. Jessica tried to block what was happening as his hands and mouth on her were rough and brutal. Adelram forced her legs apart and rubbed one of his thighs against her womanhood.

Jessica began to feel unwanted sensations over again, as in her worst nightmares. She whispered, "Please don't," one more time.

At this point, Jessica felt his fingers up and down her arms and caressing her breasts. In the next instant, Adelram lips were on her harshly, and his hand trailed down slowly and went into her slightly.

Jessica started to struggle anew, both she and Adelram knew it would fail. His taunting words prickled in her ears, "Keep
~~~

struggling, my princess. I am quite enjoying this."

Jessica froze as she felt him at her entrance, fear and dread overwhelmed her. Desperate and defeated, she whispered, "Boaz."

Upon hearing another man's name, he backhanded her and growled with anger, "You are no one else's, and I will make damn sure of it."

He squeezed her throat, and she struggled to breathe. After a short time with the lack of oxygen, she blacked out.

~~~

Adelram looked down at her for a time before slowly releasing her throat. "You will learn soon enough. I will enjoy breaking your spirit."
~~~

CHAPTER TWENTY-SIX

The silent group passed through the gate, and the shadows moved. A man dressed in black from head to toe, showing only eyes that glittered like stones, watched the group leave the city. Running in the opposite direction, the man was swift as a shadow. In no time at all, he made it to a darkened house, and stepped inside. He saw his brethren. Bowing to his future Chieftain, he spoke. "They left."

Boaz nodded his head, his orders concise. "Two roads for us to take. Sudan, or Libya. Aryan and Maaz; go to Sudan. I'll go to Libya with Salim. The first to find signs, will send a messenger. We leave before dawn."

"As you wish," responded Maaz.

They finalized their preparations. Some stayed awake, others rested. Before dawn they were ready and moved slowly out of Desert Sun as to not draw attention to themselves. When they were safely out of the city, they headed to the west where their horses were waiting. Within a minute, a hundred men split into two parties and were on their way.

Boaz's group traveled quickly in the morning hours. By the afternoon, they moved slowly in the heat, and before long, they came to an oasis. They dismounted brushed and watered the horses, and let them graze in the shade. It was a short time later, and by luck, that one of the younger warriors had tripped as he passed by the reeds. Turning to see what caused him to trip, a delicate piece of jewelry caught his attention. The warrior stood to his feet as he grabbed the anklet and swiftly made his way to Salim. He told him what he found and where. Salim quickly took the anklet and sprinted to the other side of the oasis, holding out his hand to Boaz, palms up.

Boaz took the anklet and showed it to Kontar. They nodded in silent agreement. Turning Boaz called, "Abyan, can you bring the messenger hawk?" The warrior brought over the hawk. Boaz wrote a coded message on a small paper and tied it to the leg. “Send it to Maaz," he instructed.

At the Abyan’s command, the hawk took flight. They watched until the bird was but a dot in the sky. Boaz ordered the men to saddle up, and they set off again. They made some covering from a brief sand storm, set up camp, and waited for the rest of the party. A hawk shriek was heard from above.

Abyan moved from his position and out in the open. "Here!" The hawk landed on his glove and preened its feathers. A short time later, a cloud of sand grew in the distance; then the sound of many horses as the ground rumbled. Maaz arrived, his men and horses exhausted. They rested a few more hours before setting off again around sunset.

Soon they came to an area that had plateau ledges, and they fanned out to look for any more signs. It was Boaz who found a bracelet when a torch light passed over it. With a command, they moved onwards.

They rode hard through the rest of the night, till they came to the next oasis. They gave their horses a break by the water's edge. It was here among the banks of the water's edge they found a piece of torn cloth under a rock and moved on again.

They finally came to the Nile, and it was Kontar who found the beautiful sand design. Within the picture, he noticed an arrow pattern pointing across the river. He turned his horse around and delivered the news to Boaz. The group made their way across the Nile. Boaz ordered two warriors to head to the city to scout; they had one hour.

Not even twenty minutes later. They return with a broken candle and a paper, "It was lying just outside the city gate. Boaz nodded his head and read the message. Once he finished, he raised his eyes, looked over his men, and stated in a loud voice for all to hear, "We move without stopping."

They mounted again and moved quickly toward the border into Libya. Once they reached the bottom of the plateau, they found the bracelet and raced on. Soon they made it to the next oasis and found the two dead bodies, near the nest of cobras. They moved the bodies and cremated them. Aryan moved past the cobra nest to the water to fill his canteen, and noticed something glinted in the sun. Looking closer, he saw it was a locket. He found the long pole Tony used to retrieve a snake, and went to work. With some difficulty, he managed to get the locket safely.

Aryan tossed the pole onto the fire. He turned and moved quickly toward Boaz and Kontar, who waited in the shade, both lost in thought. Approaching, Boaz turned his gaze to Aryan. Aryan held up the locket in his hand. It was Kontar's deep, inhaled breath that had caught both of their attention.

Kontar reached out and took the locket. His eyes held a worried look in them as he opened up the necklace and stared at the pictures of the inside, snapping it shut. He turned it over and noticed a crude message on the back. Staring at it for some time and tracing his fingertip over the ridges trying to make them out and slowly, he did. Kontar breathed out, "They are heading toward Aj Jaghbub. It would only make sense since it's the first city in the direction we are heading."

Boaz nodded his head thoughtfully. Boaz ordered the men to rest before the last leg of the journey. Before dawn the next day, they moved out quickly. They spotted two more dead bodies and passed around them, and they missed the small ring as it had fallen in between two rocks and laid hidden.

They soon came to a small outlying settlement. The warriors drew closer. The women by the well were frightened and ran back to the village screaming. All except for one. She dropped her jar and rushed towards them.

It was Maaz who rode ahead of his Chieftain's son and spoke, "What is it, woman?"

"Is your leader here? I have something to give him. It is imperative."

"We are pressed for time."

"I need to speak to him or Boaz."

He looked at her sharply. "How do you know that name?"

Lina babbled, "The girl, Jessica, passed through here with her aunt. And told me to give this to your leader or Boaz." Lina held out the folded paper. "Please, take it and help them."

He took the paper in his gloved fingers, turning at the sound of distant shouting. It frightened Lina, and she saw some of the men from the village coming toward them. She made a quick decision, pretended to fall, laid there and closed her eyes. She remained there until the men left.

Maaz returned to the others, and quickly they rode away. Once they were halfway to the city, only then did they slow. It was close to sunset. He handed the paper to Boaz and explained that it was from the girl.

In taking it, Boaz opened the contents and read it, and handed the necklace and paper to Kontar, who glanced at it quickly.

Kontar clutched the necklace tightly. "Save them, we must."

"We will." Responded Boaz grimly. They took off toward the city. By the time they reached the outskirts of the town, it was late at night. One of the warriors sneaked into town and scouted out the city, and within an hour, he was back and reported to the commanders.

"Tenison is high in the city. I have located most of the group at a nearby tavern but, a small force is at a hotel. I heard some of the workers talking about a young woman screaming."

Boaz and Kontar glanced at each other. Boaz silently gave commands, and they all moved quickly toward the hotel. The warriors were stopped by the management of the hotel.

"We are closed until next week."

Two of the warriors grabbed the man and pulled him inside the rest followed.

"Where are the women?" Order, Salim.

"There are no women here." Responded the man.

"Why don't I believe you?"

The man's eyes looked left to right nervously. It was here that Salim turned, shoved the man in front of him, and shot him in the chest. Salim pushed the dead body away and shot one of the men from the group they tracked. With the echo of the shots, fighting broke out. More men came out of the rooms, and the fight started in earnest.

Boaz, Kontar, Salim, and others moved up the stairs as they came to resist. The others focused on giving the two young warriors a clear way up to the last landing. Their movements synchronized as they battled, and soon they stepped onto that floor. Kontar quickly grabbed a man who jumped out from a room, slamming him into the wall, and sliced his throat.

Boaz and Kontar quickly raced down the hall, where they took care of two guards that stood outside of a door. A shot rang out and barely missed Boaz's arm. Kontar quickly turned around with fast movements, knocking the gun out of Tony's hands.

"Go!" Kontar shouted. Boaz nodded his head and turned to the door and kicked it open.

~~~

Inside the room, Adelram had been so rough with Jessica, hitting, kissing, and biting, that he left bruises all over her body. He gripped the girl's hips harshly one more time. He froze at the sound of shots and fighting outside the room.

Moving from the unconscious girl, he stood, grabbed his pants, and pulled them on loosely. He grabbed his sword and pistol. Placing the gun on the side table, he rested his sword against the bed. Adelram sat down and waited. In that short time, silence fell about the inn, and then a shot. Someone shouted. Adelram grinned with satisfaction as he turned and looked down at the girl.

He had been impressed with the fight she put up, and the girl's parents were foolish indeed for not
~~~

realizing what he truly was. Adelram's grin grew into a dark smile. *By the time they found out, it would be too late. No, his secret and that of his people would remain hidden. The claiming of the O'Willow line had begun, and the girl indeed was the key to all.*

Adelram snorted at the thought. *And yet, the so-called regent queen and protector were so naïve. No, the real threat was the late queen. Somehow the queen had kept the girl hidden. Her family was never able to talk about her until after the girl's feet left the soil of the land of her birth.*

His thoughts were interrupted, his attention turned back to the door as it seemed to shatter into pieces, the hinges hanging off the wall. He saw a young man standing in the door frame with a hardened expression, raw anger flashing in his eyes. Adelram wiped his fingers on the bedding as he slowly rose to his feet. His lip twitched with amusement as he spoke.

"They enjoyed what I did very much."

Adelram was slightly disappointed when the young man didn't rise to the bait. But

Boaz's words were enough to start the fight between them.

"I've come for the one who is mine and the other from my village."

Adelram remembered Jessica calling out another man's name; Boaz. He concluded that this could be the man.

"Well, if you want them; come and get them."

Danger filled the air, and Boaz knew only one would win this fight and take all. He stepped slowly into the room and they circled one another other trying to gauge the other's strength and weakness. Boaz flexed ever so slightly readying himself, his hand rested on the grip of his scimitar.

Boaz patiently waited and centered himself, for he saw in the older man's face and body language, the arrogance and confidence that could be his undoing. His judgment was right, not a second later, the man in front of him attacked.

Adelram charged at the young warrior and swung his sword. Boaz raised his scimitar and blocked him. Metal upon metal sounded through the room. They moved into a dangerous dance, of blocks and strikes. Adelram spotted the opening he wanted in the defenses of the other man, took the advantage, and disarmed him.

Boaz grabbed the other man's wrists and tried to force him back. He soon found himself on the floor against the bed. Movement caught their attention and turning they saw Kontar before Adelram realized what happened.

Boaz managed with one hand to grab his hidden dagger and shoved it up and into the man's diaphragm. Adelram's shock, the surprise in his eyes found Boaz before stumbling back with the blade still in his chest. Removing the dagger, it cluttered to the ground. With one hand, he reached out toward the door and with a last shudder of breath, he died.

~~~
~~~

Boaz stood with a hand on his right arm where Adelram's strike had landed. Kontar stepped over the body, after kicking him to make sure he was dead. Kontar took off his headdress and quickly worked a piece of it into a bandage. He wrapped it around his friend and prince's arm to stop the bleeding. They turned their attention to the two women.

Kontar went to Adele, first only noticing some bruising, especially around the neck and a couple of other places. He also noted the cut and bump on her head. He proceeded to check her pulse and found it stable.

Boaz's attention turned to the young girl. He was more concerned than anything. Marks and bruising littered Jessica's body. He quickly averted his eyes away; it was not proper for anyone to look upon the women like this. He found a cover on the floor and tossed it to Kontar.

Turning around, he picked the dagger up off the floor and wiped the blade clean on the dead man's pant leg. Walking back to the bed, he sliced through the ropes that bound the girl's wrists together. He wrapped Jessica in his cloak to hide her nakedness and protect her wounds. He relaxed slightly as he moved to check the pulse in her neck. Finding one, he breathed out, relieved. Quickly they gathered up the women and hurried out of the room and down the stairs. Once outside, Maaz and Aryan stepped forward and held the women for them as they mounted.

Aryan helped Boaz settle Jessica in front of him, and they all quickly raced out of the city. It was a matter of time now, and they had to make it back into Egypt and to one of their safe places hidden inside the desert.

It was right before dawn as they came back to the outskirts of the village. Standing in the road, was a man; with him the girl named Lina. Boaz raised his hand, and the group stopped. The young man stepped forward with a grim face.

"Will you take my betrothed with you? It isn't safe anymore for her."

Salim stared at the young man, and he picked up on something in his stance and eyes that gave him pause. He looked at the girl carefully, nodded to himself. As his future chieftain considered the man's request, he knew what he must do.

"Boaz, I will take the girl," said Salim.

Boaz turned his head and looked at Salim in response. Salim continued, "My wife has always wanted a girl."

Boaz closed his eyes and thought of Salim's wife, who only had two sons. Salim's wife wasn't able to have any more children. He couldn't deny them a little happiness. "Very well."

"Thank you, my prince." Whispered Salim, for Boaz only to hear him.

He moved his horse closer to the young couple. Lina turned to Faris, "I don't want to leave you."

"You must. I don't want to see you killed for an action that was honorable on your part."

"Quickly now, there isn't time before they find us gone."

Salim helped Lina up on the horse behind the man. "Faris, I love you."

"And I, you." He gave her hand one last squeeze and moved away. With that, they set off again. Lina didn't dare turn back. She buried her face into the chest of the man who had now become her father. Her other hand gently went to her stomach where she was sure that Faris' seed had taken hold.

Lina prayed now to God that it did, and she could conceive a boy to carry on his line.

~~~

Faris watched until the group was out of sight, *knowing he got an innocent out safely and prayed his line did not end. He also prayed that Lina would find happiness, asking God to send a man that could love her and their child.*
~~~

As he finished the silent prayer, his thoughts drifted to wondering how his father found out that Lina helped Jessica. He couldn't have seen her killed or worse; sold off to an abusive man as her mother had been after an infraction.

Faris moved back to the village and froze as a group of men circled him. Faris stared at his father with unwavering eyes even as the first stone hit him. Eventually, he knew no more pain and passed.

CHAPTER TWENTY-SEVEN

Boaz's group quickly made their way to the border. They ran into some military personnel. Arayan vaguely explained their situation to the sergeant, impressing the importance of returning to Egypt. The sergeant nodded his permission and the group passed through.

The leader waved them through the checkpoint, and by mid-morning, they had slowed their steeds down from a canter to a walk.

Salim spoke, "What happened for your soon-to-be-husband to give you up and put you out of your home?"

Lina stilled and pondered her words. By this time, they had neared the path to the plateau that would take them out of Libya back into Egypt. "A child had stayed hidden that I didn't see. Later that day or night, the man who is my almost Father found out."

"Almost Father?"

"Yes, my mother was married to him, but she loved another and ended up being with a child when I was born. I didn't bear a resemblance to the family."

"I see. What had become of your mother?" he asked gently.

Lina painfully swallowed as she said, "She was sold to an abusive man and didn't last a year."

"I am sorry for your loss."

"I never knew her, but I also had to be careful, and I always watched everything I did. If it weren't for Faris showing an interest in me as a future bride, my life would have been worse. But then I was caught helping the lady. That had forced Faris's hand. He came to me as I was washing clothes and pulled me away from prying eyes. He told me that I would be killed for talking to a male outside of the family, and he wouldn't let that happen. Not for an honorable."

"That is why he wanted you to be safe to spare your life."

"Yes, and possibly that of his heir, if I am with child."

She felt the warrior tense and rushed on before something happened, "He asked me to be his wife at sunset in God's eyes alone. I agreed. He was gentle but so very desperate. It wasn't until later I realized what he was trying to do when he and took me all through the night. I clung to him crying. Knowing what he was doing could cost him his life, and I felt honor-bound to help in that way. Don't think of me as a shameful harlot, for I am not. I love him dearly."

Salim didn't say anything. Just stayed silent as they moved up the cliff ledges. Stones and pebbles fell softly with each step. At one point, Lina, who was afraid of heights, looked down and squeezed her eyes tightly.

It was Salim, comforting voice that spoke when he sensed her fear, "Don't look down my daughter, you are safe."

Lina then buried her head into his shoulder and silent tears fell, for the word daughter was like a balm to her heart and soul.

After reaching the top, they veered off slightly to the south-west. Late afternoon came upon the group all too quickly, and they arrived at one of the few hidden caves. The only way they could get in was by a hidden crevice. They had to push on a specific part of the wall of the cave for it to open. They moved within the cave passage that stalactites and stalagmites sprinkled throughout the narrow passageway. The passageway slowly opened up to reveal a great space that held supplies. Three cots and bedding had been set up for the women. Lina's bed was up against the wall, the right-hand side in a corner. The other two were placed several feet away, and a makeshift curtain had gone up after Jessica, and her aunt were laid upon them.

A middle-aged warrior, named Shafi, carried some healing items behind the curtain, followed by a few others with jars and rags. Lina sat on her cot, taking all of this in and started to look around the cave. She noticed the one that called her daughter stood with four others in the middle of the room and no words spoken between them.

Shafi motioned to a younger warrior, and they exchanged words. The young one, nodded and moved to his task. He came back a few minutes later and gave some black shirts to Shafi.

Turning to Adele first, he rubbed salve into her neck and the other bruises after he bathed her and dressed her in a shirt. After this, he covered her up. Next, he cleaned the cut on her head and tended to the bump before wrapping it. Once he finished, he moved over to Jessica and unwrapped Boaz's cloak. His face went grim.

Sometime later, he stepped out from behind the curtain and taking it down he moved to the group in the center and spoke, "Lady Adele will be sore. There might also be some damage done due to the strangulation, and she might suffer due to the head injury, time will tell. Otherwise, I expect a full recovery."

"What of the girl?" asked Aryan.

"She was mishandled, but remains intact."

"What do you mean, Shafi?" It was Kontar who spoke, and his voice had a dangerous tone.

"What I mean is this, the girl had forced entry. Upon examining her, I found her barrier still in place, which is a miracle. Physically she will recover; I cannot speak for her mind or heart."

Kontar moved over to Jessica and replaced her necklace and whispered, "Princess, you and the line are safe. Rest and heal, young one."

He went to move to Adele but paused as he saw a couple of the scouts returned and spoke rapidly about an armed party not too far away from them, heading out of Libya. Kontar moved quickly out of the room. They had lost a few of their brethren already, and their bodies had already been prepared to return home once they got to the cave. Now it looked like more bloodshed was coming. Kontar knew he wanted blood and revenge.

~~~

Boaz stared after Kontar for a time, knowing he wanted blood. Others stared after the young warrior but waited for their leader, and he nodded, and they quickly followed the young warrior out of the cave. Once they were outside, they formed half circle around the party. A silent signal was given, and like shadows, they attacked quickly and quietly.

Making sure there was a safe passage for Boaz, they had reached the center of the group. The men jumped up, and before they could shout for help, guns were raised at them. Seeing their leader with a scimitar at his neck froze. Boaz's voice sounded like steel as he addressed the man in front of them, "Pray, tell me, why you decided to hunt us down?"
~~~

Despite having a scimitar at his neck growled out, “Why should we answer?”

Boaz turned to him with a stony gaze. Without warning, he slapped the man hard against the face. "The answer is clear enough; our kinswoman and her niece had been kidnapped and taken against their will. We managed to kill all that got in our way to rescue them."

One of the men whose mother was Dutch and father was Muslim, understood what was happening and why. The others had no idea what danger they were in, so the eldest spoke, hoping to ease the still angry warriors.

"We had no idea, honorable warriors. All we were told was the women had been taken forcefully by you. That you killed their husbands in cold blood. Forgive us, we only meant to avenge the women."

"You will go back to your homeland and stop tracking our movements," responded Boaz.

"We will," agreed the man.

Maaz let their leader go with such force that he falls to the ground. Just as Boaz turned to leave, the leader shot at him with a hidden pistol. If it wasn't for Kontar, who saw it at the last minute and pushed Boaz out of the way, Boaz would have been dead. The bullet grazed his upper arm. More fighting broke out, and by the time it was over, five more of their kin were killed, five injured.

Of the hundred would-be hunters turned prey, only three remained. The man that spoke and an older Muslim man who had offered no resistance were brought forward and awaited their fate. The leader's throat was slit, another that was found and hurt gravely had their wounds tightly wrapped. They placed him on a horse and tied him to it. Salim turned to the man and spoke, "He may survive if you can get him back in time. But let him also be a warning."

Happy for their lives, the two men nodded their heads. They were given only their horses and enough water to survive to the next village. Exhausted, Boaz and his warriors turned back to the hidden cave.

~~~

Adele awoke and started to panic. She tried to call out, but the only sound that left her throat was a straggled cry. Hearing her, Shafi hurried over and whispered, "Dear woman, be still you are safe."

Adele took a few deep breathes as she recognized the voice of Shafi. He helped her sit up and continued, "The young girl that was with you is safe too."

Adele turned her head, and sure enough, there was Jessica still asleep. She reached over with a trembling hand and brushed a few strands of hair from her clean but bruised face. Her fingers traced the handprint on her niece's face, and Jessica let out a soft whimper. As her eyes opened, she saw her aunt with haunted eyes that were full of pain.

Adele struggled to stand, and with the help of Shafi, moved over to Jessica's cot. She sat down on the edge of it. He walked away to get some water and some hardtack
~~~

rations. On the way back, he stopped and gave Lina some rations too.

Her voice stopped him, "Will they be alright?"

"In time, they will be, but the road will be long and hard, though."

With that, he moved quickly away and handed Adele the water and rations. She nodded her thanks, and he bowed slightly and walked away. She coaxed Jessica to eat and drink a little.

Around this time, the warrior's all returned. For a few days they stayed in the cave, resting and mending the injured. But a group of them had gone beforehand to return their brethren that had fallen back to their people. For proper burial before too much time had passed. Soon it was time for everyone else to leave, and they led Jessica and Adele carefully out of the caves.

The walk hurt Jessica, she was extremely sore and tender. When she finally reached the outside, as the sun's warming rays hit her, Jessica's legs gave out. Someone caught her. She tried to struggle, but her helper tried to reassure her. Instantly she stilled as she heard, "Let me help, woman child."

Only one person called her that, and he just did it one time. His name left her lips, "Boaz."

Jessica started to cry as everything caught up with her. Boaz quickly slipped his arms around her and under her knees and settled her on his horse. Boaz turned back and said, "Send a message to our people and let them know we are returning safely."

"Yes, my prince," answered a warrior, who grabbed the pencil and paper from the supply bag. He wrote the message and Aryan tied it to the leg of the hawk. They sent it off saying, "Go to our Chieftain, then to the rest of the commanders."

Mounting the horses, they rode quickly through the desert, only stopping when necessary. They stopped at a small oasis for a day of rest before riding on. They were only a couple of days from Midbar Shemesh now. It was here that the group would split. Adele will be going back with her people and

Jessica to the city to her adoptive siblings and her protector. Jessica was wading in the water by herself.

Jessica's arms hugged her body as tears blurred her vision, she couldn't sleep, didn't want to sleep, for she was scared. Later on, that day, her aunt pulled her into a hug and whispered, "I love you, my sweet. We will see each other soon. She pulled away and kissed her niece's head.

Smiling sadly with pain still in her eyes, Adele stared at her niece.

"Please don't leave. I will be better."

Adele froze her face had confusion in it. Adele moved back to Jessica, and she took the girl's face and her hands and placed her forehead against hers, and said, "You don't need to be better about anything. I have a family that is worried for me, and you have your own too. They all want to see us for themselves. This parting isn't goodbye."

Jessica nodded her head. Adele led her to Boaz's horse, before moving to Kontar's horse and waited. Soon the warriors were ready to leave. The larger group slowly rode toward the hidden sanctuary of their home, and the smaller group that consisted of Boaz and five others moved on toward the city with the precious burden. Jessica screamed for her aunt as the groups rode away from each other. It was no use, and she finally collapsed in silence against Boaz. Jessica finally succumbed to a fitful sleep. Boaz tightened his arms around her. *In his heart he knew there was something broken deep inside of her now, and he was filled with grief.* All Boaz could do was whisper words of comfort to her.

By the nightfall of the second day, they had reached the gates of the city. Passing through the gates and down the streets slowly, coming to the north part of the town. They stopped right outside his father's house. The other warriors dismounted and scanned the area for threats. Boaz dismounted; his attention on the sleeping woman. He reached up and slowly brought her down onto his shoulder and carrying her like that, he moved to the door and gently knocked on it as to not wake the girl.

Soon footsteps were heard, and the door opened before Quinn could exclaim with joy. It was Maaz who quickly put his hand upon her mouth and urged her inside with a harsh, "Quiet."

Aine, who had been waiting, sprang into action, motioning for Boaz to come up the steps. She hurried up before them and moved into Jessica's room where she drew a warm bath. She had Boaz lower Jessica into the tub and he left.

~~~

Aine closed the door, removed the shirt, and washed her gently from her head to her toes with help from Quinn. She helped Aine dry Jessica and dress her in a soft, loose nightgown.

Opening the door Aine, motioned Boaz to take Jessica as she put her to bed and turned down the blankets. She waited as Boaz gently laid Jessica on the bed and covered her. Aine watched him as he turned slowly, and they locked eyes. Boaz explained what he saw in the room, and what Shafi said. As he described Adelram, Aine paled ever so slightly. She grimly nodded.
~~~

It was David that spoke. "Thank you for bringing her back safely."

"Is there anything we can do to return the favor?" asked Quinn.

Boaz's lips quirked a little into a sad smile, "Yes, let me sit beside the girl tonight."

David went to protest, but Aine hushed him. She understood why Boaz proposed the offer. She ushered the other two out of the room, and as she shut the door, she whispered, "Goodnight."

~~~

By early morning of the next day Jessica sat up, gasping in fear. It was Boaz's voice that calmed her struggles.

"You are a safe, woman child; back in my father's home. Aine and David are here for you along with that girl. I need to tend to
~~~

some pressing duties. I'll come back as soon as I'm finished."

"Please don't leave. I don't want to lose you like Adele."

Boaz sank to his knees and took her hands in his. He kissed her fingertips and stroked her hair with his other hand. His eyes were full of emotions he couldn't disguise. He bit them back and smiled tenderly. "You are not losing your aunt, nor will you lose me. You will never lose me. You're a part of me, somehow. Try to rest; before you know it, I'll be back."

"Promise me." Jessica's voice trembled.

"I promise. I will send Aine up with some food; please try to eat for me." Standing, Boaz kissed Jessica's forehead and reluctantly walked out of the room. Clenching his fists, he left the door open slightly and made his way downstairs. Entering the sitting room, he saw his father and the guests there.

"The girl is awake, and I suggest a light breakfast, nothing heavy for her stomach." Aine stood up and moved out of the room without a word. Boaz and his father stared at each other for a time. Finally, Boaz spoke. "I take my leave, Father."

"Very well, my son. May God protect you." Boaz bowed slightly and walked out of the house. He met with the others, mounted his horse, and they rode off.

CHAPTER TWENTY-EIGHT

It was now the nineteenth of December the year 1837. It had been seven months since Jessica, and her aunt were rescued. Jessica barely left her room. When she did, she was quiet, reserved, and had difficulties expressing herself when she spoke. She barely ate anything unless Boaz coaxed her, and her weight dropped to a dangerous level.

Jessica almost translucent skin emphasized her ribcage, and the dark circles around her eyes gave her corpse like appearance. She cried every day, even when he was there, breaking down at the oddest of times. On many nights, she lay awake, afraid to sleep. When she did, her dreams were horrible and vivid images; fleeting nightmares that stayed with her when she awoke.

Today, the sound of thunder roused Jessica, but Boaz was nowhere to be seen. She watched the window as lightning flashed again. The storm suited Jessica just fine. It was winter in Egypt, and most of their rainfall happened during this time from November to April.

Jessica slowly got up from the bed and moved to the window and sat down on the window seat. She placed her head on the glass and closed her eyes, trying to figure out what else had awakened her. She felt like something was going to happen, and it wouldn't be right. Maybe a bath would help clear the fog in her mind.

Jessica went into the bathroom and bathed. While the warmth of the water and lavender incense was calming, no revelations came to her. Wrapping herself up in a bath blanket, she shuffled to the dresser.

Jessica watched herself take out lingerie. She then proceeded to open another drawer and pulled out a gray cotton nightgown. The collar and cuffs of the gown were ruffled, the hem gathered in pools at her feet. It had a hand-gathered smocking with pearly shell buttons down the front of it.

Jessica's lips twitched into a sad half-smile as she slipped into the clothes. At least she could take comfort in the soothing way the gown hugged her body. She ran her brush through her damp hair but had to stop halfway through for the motion took more energy than she could muster. Lightning flashed through the room again. Jessica decided maybe a change of scenery would help ease her distress. She moved out of the bedroom and down the hall.

Halfway down the steps, Jessica froze upon hearing many voices coming from the sitting room. She blinked a few times, her breathing heavy, as she slowly began backing up the steps, despite the fact she saw two of Boaz's men standing at the bottom. Perhaps he intended to come see her when they were finished speaking. She paused at the sound of a woman's words.

"As I said, my son is close to our lady's age and will be a perfect match."

Aine's voice drifted to her. "A perfect match? Don't make me laugh, Priscilla. It would be the worst thing that can happen."

"And yet, it is the only thing we can do to keep the line safe," murmured another person whose voice Jessica didn't recognize.

At that, she heard Boaz, scoff.

They were deciding her future without so much as asking her opinion. Anger pulsed new energy through her limbs, and she hurried down the stairs. She glared at the two warriors, and they stepped aside. Bursting into the room, Jessica looked around, her fingers gripping her nightgown; an attempt at self-comfort.

For a split second, Jessica scanned the room, her gaze resting on Boaz. He sat in an armchair, legs stretched lazily in front of him and crossed at the ankle. He leaned on his left arm, temple resting on his forefinger. He had an aire of boredom about him, until he saw Jessica and sat upright. He was pleased to see her out of her room, albeit in a nightgown. Jessica was too angry to see the slight smile curl his lip.

Aine stood. "Jessica!"

All eyes in the room zeroed in on her.

Jessica's face was flushed, and her body trembled. She shrieked at the group, "How dare you!" Her response bewildered everyone. Taking a deep breath, she began again. "How dare you! How dare you sit there discussing my life! You have no right in that regard! None! If anyone does, it would be Aine and David! They have been there since the beginning with me! The rest of you have not!"

Priscilla opened her mouth to speak, but Jessica snapped, "No. I will not marry your son. I don't even know him! You are completely insane even to think that!"

"It's for your safety!" Priscilla said sternly.

Boaz, watched intently.

Jessica and Priscilla locked eyes. Silence took over the room as Jessica tried to keep standing tall. But a tear slid down her cheek.

She looked away, her gaze meeting Boaz's again.

Adele's voice drifted through her head, and it seemed like a lifetime ago. '*She will need your help, Boaz, and the strength that not only runs through your veins but of our people as well. I am asking you not only as of the future Chieftain of our people but also as a warrior.'*

Jessica closed her eyes and thought for a moment, *Boaz is a royal and a warrior, he would have the power to help me, is it true.* She sucked her lip in, thought deeply, and she realized what she needed to do. Releasing her lip, she steeled her resolve, finding strength she never knew she had. *I'll go before him, as Queen Esther did before King Xerxes.* Jessica took a deep breath, and despite the trembling, took in the faces staring at her. She noticed Brian kept looking at Aine, worry glistening in his eyes. "I see now," Jessica murmured, turning to face Boaz.

"I told you all that she would see reason," Pricilla gloated.

Priscilla's smug tone echoed loudly in Jessica's ears. She kept her gaze focused on

Boaz. He straightened some more and raised an eyebrow, intrigued by her behavior. Jessica moved toward him till she stood in front of him. Boaz leaned forward in the way he always did to let her know that she had his full attention. "Boaz Stern, are you not the future Chieftain of your people?"

"I am." Boaz's words came out deceptively calm and quiet.

Jessica bit her lip and thought of her next words as she remembered Queen Esther. Her heart pounded so hard against her chest; Jessica was afraid everyone saw through her shallow confidence. Boaz exchanged a quick glance with a few of his brethren. As tension hung in the air around them, it seemed as if time stood still.

A loud crack of thunder sounded through the room, and it made everyone jump. It was enough for Jessica to make her move, and she dropped to her knees. She knelt prostrate, and forehead touching the ground. Her voice trembled as she asked, "I have a petition and request for you, My Lord."

Her trepidation confused him, but he answered, "What is your petition and request, princess?"

Jessica took another deep breath and looked up. "My petition is to live my life. My request is my freedom."

Acknowledgments

I want to say thank you to God, first and foremost. For the inspiration to write this and the courage to share the story.

Second, I want to thank Joshua James Imagines for the beautiful ocean scene that I was allowed to use for the background of my book cover.

Third, I want to thank my friend, Laura Luikart, for bringing the idea for my book cover to life.

Fourth, I want to thank a dear friend and editor, Heidi Owens for revising, A Hidden Danger. You rock girl!

Fifth, I want to thank two of my dearest best friends in the world who are truly amazing, Carol Drury and Mark Williams, thank you for believing in me throughout the years we've known and each other. And for the push needed to make this happen.

Your friendship and love are always in my heart.

Sixth, I want to thank my aunt, Susan Shreve, for the continued encouragement to keep writing this even when I felt it was hopeless.

Seventh, I want to thank my parents, John and Kathy Woodcock, and my grandmother, Eleanor Scowden for their unconditional love and support.

Eighth, I want to thank Heidi Owens, Tiffany Warren, Sonya DiPietro, Melissa Gard, and Jennifer Woodcock. You all have been truly remarkable friends, and sisters and your continued love and support means the world to me.

Lastly, for anyone who is not mentioned but had a hand in helping me with the information I needed or insight, thank you all from the bottom of my heart.

References:

Chapter 7

Midbar is the Hebrew word for desert.

Shemesh is the Hebrew word for sun.

Source: Goodman, M. (1994). Let's learn Hebrew picture dictionary. Lincolnwood, IL, USA: Passport Books.

Chapter 9

Scriptures: Jonah 4: 4, Psalm 37: 8, Matthew 6:14

(Are from the NLT, unless otherwise stated)

Chapter 22

Egyptian Cobra- Cleopatra's Snake. Retrieved July 2013, https://dinoanimals.com/animals/egyptian-cobra-cleopatras-snake/

Chapter 23

Ta'amiya (Falafel) is a dish that originated in Egypt.

Source: Typical Food of Egypt. (n.d). Retrieved from http://www.egypt.cl/typical-food.htm

Chapter 28

The book of Queen Esther was the inspiration for this chapter.

About the Author

Nicole Marie Woodcock lives in Guys Mills, Pennsylvania. She has an Associate's Degree in psychology.

Nicole loves to read. She enjoys being creative. She loves to write and spends much time daydreaming. She cares for those around her and the environment.

With this book, she hopes she can let others know they are not alone in what they are going through. We all have a lot of hidden truths within; there is always hope and someone out there who understands. People do care and love us. Also, she hopes to take you, the reader, on a unique journey to find that truth.

Made in the USA
Middletown, DE
12 April 2021